"Friends, right?"

"With or without sex?"

Mallory sighed.

Gunner smiled slowly. "Okay," he said, releasing her arm and offering his hand. "No sex."

The second she grasped his hand, he tugged her into his arms.

She felt so good against him, warm and soft and real. He lowered his mouth to hers, and their tongues touched. A soft, helpless moan came from the back of her throat, lighting a fire in his belly that tested his self-control.

If he got any harder he was going to explode.

A firm shove to his chest sent him back a step.

"What's wrong with you?" Mallory glared at him. "We just agreed to be friends, no sex."

"Kissing isn't sex."

She was breathing hard, her breasts rising and falling. Gunner tried not to stare. Or think about how sweet she'd tasted.

God, he wanted her...and he'd do whatever it took to get her back in his bed.

Dear Reader,

Welcome to all of you who are new to my Made in Montana series! As for the rest of you "old-timers," you'll be surprised at some of the changes around Blackfoot Falls.

Right before starting this book, I was thinking about a few of the characters we've met and others whose stories I want to tell, and it hit me. I've been an absolute terrible hostess. There are only two places where people can eat and drink in the whole town. That might've been fine after the economy tanked and before the McAllisters opened the dude ranch, but too much has happened since then.

Kids who went off to college or set out to see the world have been coming home. Tourism is on the rise, and Hollywood's renewed interest in Westerns has brought film crews to capture the beautiful, untamed land at the foot of the Rockies.

I couldn't have everyone rebelling and moving to Kalispell, so I had to do something quick. California bar owner Mallory Brandt seemed like a good candidate to stir things up on Main Street. The night she opens the Full Moon Saloon, Gunner Ellison, her best friend—and the one man she never should've had sex with—shows up, determined to win her back.

There's a special place in my heart for this couple, even with all the trouble they gave me. I hope you enjoy their story.

All my best,

Debbi Rawlins

Debbi Rawlins

——

Come Closer, Cowboy

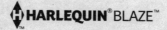

Recycling programs
for this product may
not exist in your area.

ISBN-13: 978-0-373-79896-4

Come Closer, Cowboy

Copyright © 2016 by Debbi Quattrone

Printed in U.S.A.

www.Harlequin.com

Debbi Rawlins grew up in the country and loved Western movies and books. Her first crush was on a cowboy—okay, he was an actor in the role of a cowboy, but she was only eleven, so it counts. It was Houston, Texas, where she first started writing for Harlequin, and now she has her own ranch... of sorts. Instead of horses, she has four dogs, four cats, a trio of goats and free-range cattle on a few acres in gorgeous rural Utah.

Books by Debbi Rawlins

Harlequin Blaze

Made in Montana

Barefoot Blue Jean Night
Own the Night
On a Snowy Christmas Night
You're Still the One
No One Needs to Know
From This Moment On
Alone with You
Need You Now
Behind Closed Doors
Anywhere with You
Come On Over
This Kiss

To get the inside scoop on Harlequin Blaze and its talented writers, be sure to check out BlazeAuthors.com.

All backlist available in ebook format.

Visit the Author Profile page at Harlequin.com for more titles.

1

MALLORY HAD DISAPPEARED. Without a single word. Without so much as leaving a voice mail.

Gunner Ellison stood at the open door to the Renegade and slipped off his sunglasses. He'd expected to see her standing behind the bar just like always, staring back at him with those sexy green eyes and that killer smile. But the place was empty. The solid oak tables and chairs were gone. So was the pool table, the jukebox and the dartboard. In the window was a sign that said Closed for Good.

Too many sleepless nights and the long plane ride had nearly knocked him on his ass. Exhausted, Gunner rubbed his eyes, hoping this was nothing but a bad dream. Then he took another bleak look around.

Everything. Gone.

He just didn't get it. She still had another week left on her lease. They'd talked about her raising drink prices in order to meet the steep rent hike. Other stuntmen he worked and drank with, and even the bikers who crowded her Valencia bar at all hours, none of them would've cared. Not if it meant keeping Mallory in business.

This was crazy. They were friends, damn it, and he'd offered to help her. Couldn't she have waited for him to get back before giving up the place?

He'd been working on location in Argentina for four weeks. They'd talked a couple times after he'd first gotten there. But then she'd stopped taking his calls. And he had a terrible feeling he knew why.

They'd had sex. In the back room the night before he'd left. On the pool table, against the wall and maybe even on the old oak bar itself.

They'd both had a few drinks, though he hadn't been too drunk when he'd pulled her into his arms. Maybe she'd been more wasted than he'd thought—she rarely had more than a beer around closing time—but something about that night had made them wild for each other. Tearing at each other's clothes. Slow, deep kisses until neither of them could breathe. He'd tried to figure it out. Every night as he'd lain awake, remembering the taste of her, or the way she'd moaned.

"Can I help you, mister?" An older man wearing stained work clothes and mopping his bald head came from the back room.

"Any idea when the Renegade closed?"

"We started remodeling over a week ago. Got called at the last minute."

Gunner swept a final gaze around the room. For ten years he'd been coming here. The place held a lot of memories, not just of Mallory. He'd felt like he belonged here after he'd gotten his shot in the stunt business. Coop, Mallory's dad, had been a stuntman himself, hurt bad before he opened the bar. But he and the other guys who'd hung out at the Renegade had made Gunner, a damn rookie in the Stuntmen's Association, feel like one of them.

Mallory had taken over the day after Coop's funeral. It was going on six years now, but the place had been her home since her mother had run off.

"Well, mister, I'm afraid you're gonna have to leave. It's quitting time and I'm locking up."

Gunner nodded. He'd forgotten the guy was there.

Pulling out his phone, he headed for his truck. He tried Mallory. And was sent straight to voice mail. She was really starting to piss him off.

He drove to her apartment on Rye Canyon, anger simmering in his gut. He was too exhausted for this bullshit. So they'd had sex. Didn't mean they had to avoid each other.

Though he'd never been inside, he knew her unit was on the ground floor at the end. He didn't see her car and cruised past a U-Haul truck that was blocking his view.

Gunner slowed when he saw a young woman with dark hair carrying a box into the apartment. Mallory's apartment. His heart jumped a few gears and shot into overdrive.

When the woman emerged and headed to the U-Haul, Gunner lowered his window. "Excuse me. A friend of mine used to live in your apartment. Do you have any idea where she moved?"

She paused a moment. "I think Montana."

Montana? What the hell? Who did Mallory know in—

Shit. "Hey, thanks," he said, and pulled out. At the next corner, he stopped and grabbed his phone.

He didn't have many people on speed dial, but Ben Wolf was one of them. If Mallory had moved to Montana it was because of their friend Wolf. After Gunner got some answers, then maybe he'd be able to get a good night's sleep. Without dreaming of Mallory's long, slender legs wrapped around his waist.

"Is THERE ANY chance at all you can still get here by this evening?" Mallory Brandt asked, then held the phone a foot away from her ear. The man had to be near deaf. His voice was so loud she could've heard him from the back room.

"No, ma'am. It's my truck," Dexter said. "The brakes are shot. Gotta get them replaced."

"Okay." Granted, she knew nothing about cars, but she suspected his brakes hadn't suddenly crapped out without warning. When she'd responded to his ad for the used mechanical bull, Dexter had promised he could deliver it by today. "So, that means…what?"

"Mebbe you can borrow a vehicle and pick Fanny up yourself," Dexter said, a shrewd dip in his tone. "I'll knock off forty bucks."

Mallory rubbed her bloodshot eyes. So that's what this was about…he'd decided he didn't want to drive the seventy miles to Blackfoot Falls. "Not possible," she said, wondering if he knew that a bull was male. "New brakes can't be cheap. Maybe *you* can borrow another truck and deliver Fanny. That way you'll have money to pay for your repair."

Dexter sighed. "Mebbe tomorrow."

"Let me know." She disconnected the call and kept her cussing to a low murmur.

She was alone in the front of the bar. Mike, the finish carpenter, was tending to a few details in the back where the bull would be set up. If the stupid thing ever made it. Damn, she'd really wanted it here for opening tonight.

Oh, well, she'd been warned that people operated at a slower pace here in northwest Montana. She shouldn't let a minor delay annoy her. Everything had gone smoothly with the renovations. The big old saloon had sat empty and neglected for fifteen years according to Sadie, who owned the Watering Hole, the only other bar for miles, and who was also the mayor.

When Mallory had questioned the need for another drinking establishment, she was assured she'd have all the business she could handle. Things were looking up in the small town. The ranchers who'd suffered from the poor economy had begun hiring men again. Other changes in the area had brought some tourism, and a film crew was shooting a Western miniseries around the foothills of the Rocky Mountains.

After three weeks, she was still in awe of them. Of course she'd seen the Rockies many times in movies and in photos. But here, all she had to do was step outside the bar for a perfect view of the snowcapped peaks unfazed by the July heat.

No wonder the area drew directors and location scouts—with a little help from Ben, an ex-stuntman she'd gotten to know at the Renegade. He'd quit stunt work to buy a ranch and raise movie stock. He'd talked up the beauty of Montana and word had spread.

Kind of ironic, Mallory thought as she skimmed her hand over the newly varnished oak bar, that she had come fourteen hundred miles to get away from Hollywood and it just might be those same folks who'd keep her in business.

No, not true. She hadn't been trying to escape Hollywood. Just Gunner. And ridiculous California rents. Mostly Gunner, though.

God, she was such an idiot.

If she hadn't wanted to, there wouldn't have been enough tequila in the world to get her so drunk she'd have sex with him. Though she'd had no problem letting him think otherwise. But yes, she'd known exactly what she was getting herself into, and she'd done it anyway. Just yanked off her shirt. Let him peel off her jeans, then helped him pull down his.

And then she'd been in his arms, his strong, muscled arms, being lifted onto the pool table, his hot, demanding mouth making her his slave. Not for life. She had some pride.

But holy hell.

The very least he could've done was be a lousy kisser. How easily she could've pushed him away then. Kissing was key. If a guy didn't pass that test, he was dead to her.

Wow, but Gunner... What he could do with that clever mouth of his...

She gulped in a lungful of air. Great. She was getting warm just thinking about it. Which wasn't good considering she'd been trying very hard to forget that night.

She picked up the piece of notebook paper with her formidable to-do list on it and fanned herself. No use pining over him. Gunner was the type of man who belonged to all women, not just one. She'd known that even before she'd snatched that forbidden taste. And he didn't seem to mind taking advantage of the many offers slipped to him with a whisper or a glance, a blatant invitation.

In all fairness, she had to admit he never encouraged the attention. But at six foot two with those broad shoulders, wavy dark hair and that sexy baritone, women took notice.

Basically, he was one of those rare and fortunate men who didn't have to work at being hot. Yes, he took fitness seriously, but keeping in shape went with his job.

Well, she didn't have to worry about Gunner popping in and catching her off guard, or watching women throwing themselves at him anymore, now, did she?

Sighing, Mallory glanced around her new bar with equal parts satisfaction, anxiety and sadness. By working at a breakneck pace since day one, she'd fallen into bed each night too exhausted to allow for second thoughts.

But she had a few lurking in the back of her mind. While her LA customers weren't really friends, they were her *people*. She'd known many of the old scoundrels her whole life. And she missed them. Missed the same stupid jokes they'd told a million times, missed the teasing winks and good-natured arguing over darts or cards.

And she'd disappointed all of them. She knew that for a fact, and it hurt. Because all of this was her fault. No, she couldn't have afforded the new rent, but she hadn't even shopped around for a new place in the area or explored other options.

Whether or not she adjusted to life in Blackfoot Falls she was here to stay. She'd sunk everything she had into this place.

All because she'd crossed a line that night, a line she could never uncross. And now she wanted Gunner with a burning ache that wouldn't ease. Her only hope was that time and distance would cure what was seriously ailing her. And if she was really lucky, she'd stop feeling so shitty for not returning his calls.

"Things must be going well if you've got time to stand there gathering wool." Sadie had slipped in without Mallory hearing the door. Which meant Mike must've oiled the hinges. The man was a godsend. Sadie frowned. "You poor child. You don't even know what that means."

"Yes, I do. I was just…" Mallory sighed. "I don't know what I was doing. I'm probably in shock. If I pass out can I count on the honor system tonight?"

Sadie chuckled. "Everything looks real nice," she said, inspecting the room, her gaze lingering on the Full Moon Saloon banner Mallory had put up above the mirrors behind the bar and, right under that, a sign that said No Fighting, or You Will Be Banned. Sadie smiled with approval. She might look like a classic grandma. Inside she was made of pure steel. "I'm glad you brought those oak tables and chairs with you. They match the bar like they were made for each other. I see the jukebox and pool table got here. What about the mechanical bull?"

"No." Mallory pressed her lips together to stop a curse. Even though she'd heard Sadie cut loose on a cocky young cowboy at the Watering Hole.

"That might not be a bad thing," Sadie said. "I'm guessing you'll have all you can handle tonight. Who have you got coming in?"

"Elaine. She's the only waitress I hired."

"Oh, honey, my place is half this size and I have three gals. You'll be plenty busy, I can guarantee you that."

"My old bar was about the size of the Watering Hole and I worked mostly by myself. Pouring, serving, you name it. But I'm pretty quick."

Sadie gave her a dry look.

"No offense."

She just smiled.

Mallory guessed the woman was about the same age as her mom. But Sadie had done more for her in the past three weeks than Mallory's mother had seen fit to do in the twelve years she'd bothered to stick around.

"Sadie, have I told you how much I appreciate what you—"

"Yes. About a hundred times. Now hush." Sadie gestured at the floor. "Lord knows how you put a little gleam in that pine but it won't last long. Have you noticed some of the boots on these cowboys? I had to put down heavy-duty mats." She snorted. "They wouldn't stop three seconds to stomp off the dry mud."

Mallory grinned. "I bet you didn't let them get away with that."

"Hell, no. I refused to serve them."

"Now, I sure hope you're not talking about me, Mayor Thompson," Mike said, coming from the back room with a loose stride and an easy smile.

Sadie turned to look at him. "Don't you Mayor Thompson me, young man. Sorriest decision of my life, running for office. I should've let that old windbag Leland keep the damn job."

"Then where would we be? He would've shot down the Hollywood people. You're helping the town make some money without letting it be overrun."

"You two might be the only folks who believe that."

"Lots of people are on your side, Sadie." Mike unbuckled his tool belt. "It's the naysayers making all the noise. Nothing new there. I need to grab some lunch. You wanna come, Mallory? I know you haven't eaten." He glanced at Sadie. "You, too. I'm buying."

Mallory pressed a hand to her nervous tummy. "No, thanks."

Mike looked as if he was about to argue, then reconsidered. "Sadie?"

"No, but I'll walk you out. I've got a meeting in five minutes." She studied Mallory. "At least let Mike bring something back for you. The day is just gonna get crazier."

"I know, but I have a hundred new glasses to wash and stack," she said, ripping open the box sitting in front of her and grinning. "I've gathered enough wool for now."

Sadie laughed. "Then we'll just get out of your way," she said and prompted Mike to go ahead of her. As soon as he turned for the door, she glanced back and mouthed, "He's single."

And sweet as pie.

So Mallory had heard. From Louise, who owned the fabric and craft store, along with her friend Sylvia. Also from the Lemon sisters, twins in their eighties, who were as cute as could be...when they weren't arguing.

She pulled out a set of glasses and got another glimpse of Mike before the door closed. He was tall, good-looking and the most easygoing man she'd ever met. He owned a ranch but when times had gotten tough, he'd picked up carpentry jobs to make ends meet. Recently he'd gone back to raising cattle full-time. Yes, she was paying him for the work, but he was doing her a favor.

Mike really was a terrific guy.

He just wasn't Gunner.

2

AT 6:00 MALLORY opened the heavy wooden doors of the Full Moon Saloon. She was officially open for business and damned if Sadie hadn't been right. A dozen people were already waiting on the sidewalk.

Mostly cowboys, three of them chatting up guests from the Sundance dude ranch. She didn't know that for a fact, but the women who tended to stay there were pretty easy to spot.

"Come on in," she said. "Your first drink is on the house."

A couple of energetic hoots made her smile as she stepped out of the way. They wasted no time filing inside, so she started for her post behind the bar while checking out the footwear. The men's boots were clean—some looked new. All except for the short dusty cowboy who ignored the women and went straight for a barstool.

Yep, he would be the one who screwed up her floor.

Elaine was already filling pitchers with beer by the time Mallory got herself stationed by the bowls of garnish. The lemons and limes were cut into wedges. Sadie warned she'd go through the limes quickly. As for the olives and cherries, Mallory stocked only a couple bottles of each.

Although she really hoped she wouldn't need them. Beer and shots had been the staples at the Renegade. Gin and tonic, rum and Coke, the obvious drinks were no problem. But her knowledge of fancy cocktails was shaky at best.

"Who wants pitchers?" Elaine yelled so loud, Mallory nearly jumped out of her jeans.

Several hands went up.

Mallory had wondered how the waitress had taken orders so fast, not that she minded the casual approach. It was comforting, actually. If she closed her eyes she could've been back home. After Elaine loaded her tray, Mallory took over the tap and filled a mug for the guy sitting at the bar.

"Hey, cool name. I love Full Moon Saloon." A petite blonde walked up and leaned against the bar as she studied the bottles of liquor on the shelves behind Mallory.

She still wasn't sure about the name. Days after she'd come up with it and tested it on Ben and Sadie, Mallory had recognized the subconscious link to Gunner. To that fateful night. She'd specifically remembered the moon was full because of her desperate attempt to explain her stupid error in judgment. Lots of crazy stuff happened on nights with full moons. Ask any cop.

"Let's see…" The blonde leaned closer, squinting at the bottles of flavored tequila. "Do you have Jell-O shots?"

Mallory held in a groan.

"Oh, for God's sake, this is our first night. Give us a break," Elaine said as she returned to fill more pitchers. "Order a real drink."

The blonde's eyes widened.

Mallory had to look away. With her fickle mood, if she started laughing there was no telling when she'd stop. Of course she'd liked the thirtysomething waitress—that's why she'd hired her. But she liked Elaine twice as much now.

"You must be related to Sadie," Mallory muttered under her breath while reaching around Elaine for her order ticket.

She grinned. "I'll take that as a compliment."

"Yep."

"Um, excuse me," the blonde said, and feeling duly ashamed—the woman was a customer, after all—Mallory gave her a smile. "Could you define 'real drink'?"

Mallory tried not to look at Elaine. She really did. But their eyes met, briefly, and that was all it took. A laugh tickled the bottom of her throat as it forced its way up. For crying out loud, she wasn't the giddy type. Exhaustion and nerves were to blame.

She had to get a grip. Another dozen or so people had entered the bar. They would never catch up if she didn't put an end to this foolishness.

"How about a margarita?" Mallory asked the blonde who was looking impatient.

"Frozen?" she asked with a hopeful smile.

Mallory sighed. "Sure," she said and nodded at the cowboy with the filthy boots, who was motioning for another beer.

For the next two hours, she and Elaine were so slammed they didn't have time to look at each other, much less speak. Good thing. If Elaine had a moment to think she'd probably quit. And Mallory wouldn't blame her. Every time the door opened, Mallory cringed. She sure didn't need any more business tonight. Or any other night until she hired additional help.

Ten minutes and a dozen margaritas later, she took a quick gulp of cold water and straightened her back. She'd been hunched over the blender for most of the evening. Why had she suggested a margarita? Of course it became the popular choice of the night. For the women mostly. Thank God for beer-drinking cowboys.

Using the back of her wrist she pushed the hair off her face. So much for her nice, neat ponytail. She looked up just as the door opened and saw it was Ben and Grace. Awesome. Mallory had no qualms about putting Ben to work until they were caught up. She liked his girlfriend and might've hit her up, too, but Grace was the sheriff. Asking her to serve drinks didn't seem kosher.

Mallory caught their attention and motioned them over. Ben responded with a nod. The smile of relief died on her lips when she saw the dark-haired man directly behind them. Her heart jumped wildly.

Gunner?

Couldn't be.

Her heart was pounding so hard she could barely breathe. The glass she was holding almost slipped through her trembling fingers before she set it down.

How was this possible? He knew Ben, sure. Probably better than she did. They'd worked together sometimes and occasionally drank at the Renegade. But they were both loners and to call them friends would be a stretch. Or that's what she'd thought.

Dammit. She didn't need this, not now. Not ever.

They were making their way through the crowd, lingering here and there, when someone stopped to chat with Ben or Grace. But Gunner, from the second his eyes found hers, hadn't looked away once. He just kept staring, his mouth curved in a tight smile that lowered her body temperature by ten degrees.

He needed a haircut and he clearly hadn't shaved in several days. His face looked darker, from weeks in the hot Argentinian sun. Or from anger, maybe.

Goddamn Ben. Why hadn't he said anything to her?

She pretended to mess with the blender, using it as an excuse to stare down while she struggled for composure.

"Excuse me? May I get some quarters?" It was the same blonde who'd started the run on frozen margaritas. She laid a five on the bar. "For the jukebox."

Quarters. Mallory dried her unsteady hands. She had a tin of them somewhere. The hell with it. She opened the register and dug out some coins. "Here you go," she said, stacking them on the five-dollar bill. "Keep your money."

"Really? Thanks." The woman scooped them into her palm, then turned and bumped into Gunner. "Oh," she said, tilting her head back to look up at him. "Hello."

Without a word, he stepped back to give her more room, his gaze remaining locked on Mallory.

"Go ahead. You can have him, too," Mallory said, as they played the staring game.

The blonde giggled. Gave a breathless sigh. Did the hair toss. Moistened her lips.

Yep, Gunner Ellison was in the house.

Of course Ben had always received his fair share of female attention, as well. But Grace carried a gun so it probably wasn't much of a problem in Blackfoot Falls.

After an awkward silence, the woman slipped away. Ben and Grace left a couple who'd stopped them and were headed for the bar.

Tension cramped Mallory's neck and shoulders, but she refused to break eye contact with Gunner.

Jesus, one of them had to say something.

"What a surprise seeing you here," she said finally, just as Grace slid onto a barstool at the end of the bar.

"I'm sure it is." His cool assessment didn't waver. Oh, he was pissed, all right.

"Hey." Mallory turned to smile at Grace. And then Ben when he came up behind Grace and put his hands on her shoulders. Even though he was a traitor and they'd have words later. No. He couldn't have known.

"Wow, you're busy," Grace said. "Please. Just ignore us."

"She will." Gunner leaned an elbow on the bar and gave her a lazy smile. "Mallory's good at that."

"I need drinks over here," Elaine called out from the tap at the other end, her patience clearly slipping.

"Sorry." Mallory hurried over, embarrassed to see the waitress busting ass filling mugs and pitchers, and scooping up glasses of ice. Mallory glanced at the first two drink tickets and grabbed bottles of tequila and rum from the shelf.

Dammit, she'd planned to ask for Ben's help, though she wouldn't now. Better he keep his guest busy and away from her.

She poured two shots, head bent, letting loose strands of hair hide part of her face before she slid a look down the bar.

Gunner wasn't there.

Where the hell—?

"Move over." His rough palm on her arm made her jump. "I'll get the mixed drinks."

"No, thanks," she said, refusing to budge. "We're fine."

Elaine turned her awestruck look from Gunner to glare at Mallory. The message was clear—*Accept his offer or I'll kill you in your sleep.*

"Fine." Mallory barely got the word out before he'd put his hands on her hips and moved her over a foot.

He set the drink tickets in a row so he could easily read them, lined up glasses, for both cocktails and shots, dispensed ice cubes in one fluid motion, then went to work pouring and mixing.

As soon as Elaine left with her loaded tray, Mallory took over the tap. She told herself that standing near him was nothing. How many times had he helped her on busy nights at the Renegade? Fifty? Sixty times? Probably more.

Except, back then, they hadn't had sex yet. She hadn't known the hot, bone-melting feel of his mouth on hers, or experienced the sweet rough texture of his tongue as he licked a path to her breasts.

And then making her wait. And wait. Her tightened nipple aching so badly she'd thought she would go crazy before he finally sucked it into his mouth.

After that he'd kind of lost it, too, impatiently stripping off her panties then lowering his mouth…

Mallory shifted her weight from one foot to the other. She exchanged a filled mug for an empty one and pressed an ice cube to her throat. "It's hot in here," she muttered.

He gave her a faintly mocking smile.

"Shut up, Gunner. I mean it."

Beer foamed over the mug's rim and spilled onto her hand. It took two tries for her to shut off the tap. She swallowed a string of curses as she grabbed a clean rag and mopped up.

"Excuse me." A pretty redhead was looking at Gunner. "What nights will the band play?"

"Ask the boss," he said, nodding at Mallory.

"I haven't found one yet, and the stage needs more work. But I'm hoping to have live music soon."

"Thanks." The redhead didn't care. She'd only wanted an excuse to talk to Gunner.

It was a familiar scenario. Women were always drawn to him. Mallory hated that she cared.

"You have dartboards in the back, but I don't see any darts." Again, the woman addressed Gunner, then leaned over the bar for a look. "Do you have some back there?"

Mallory doubted she'd find them behind Gunner's fly.

He kept pouring drinks but glanced at Mallory. "Sweetheart, where are the darts?"

She sucked in a breath. "Right here," she said, and stooped to open a lower cabinet. He'd never called her that before, and she didn't know what game he was playing. She straightened and handed over the box of darts. "Sorry about that."

A look of disappointment on the other woman's face cheered Mallory, making her twice the fool. If Gunner had intended to mislead the redhead, it was only because he wasn't interested. Or he had his eye on someone else.

Mallory glanced around the room. Lots of pretty women had turned out, mostly in pairs or groups. And now some of them were starting to line up at the bar to get their drinks directly from Gunner. Great. Just great.

After she filled two pitchers, she walked over to Ben and Grace, who had settled in. They were busy talking to people but she felt bad she hadn't even offered them a drink.

She waited for a break in the conversation and asked, "What can I get you guys?"

"Don't worry about us," Grace said, at the same time Ben said, "Beer."

Grace leaned back and gave him a look.

"Hey, I was going to offer to help," he said. "But it's too crowded back there. At least Gunner seems to know what he's doing."

Mallory hesitated. "I can't believe you didn't tell me he was coming."

"He wanted to surprise you."

"Ah." She knew what kind of beer Ben drank and got a bottle from the fridge. "Grace? Beer? Wine? I have both red and white, but they're just okay."

"Beer's fine," Grace said, and grabbed Ben's bottle before he could.

He just grinned and stole a kiss.

Mallory couldn't help smiling. They were the most adorable couple. Ben had changed. She didn't know whether it was because of Grace or Blackfoot Falls, or maybe it was a combination of the two, but he seemed more relaxed, certainly happier.

Something made her turn her head. Gunner was watching her. She lost the sappy smile and got a second beer from the fridge. Before she twisted off the cap she said, "Grace, maybe you'd like Gunner to make you a mai tai?"

"A what?"

"Or some fancy blended drink."

Ben laughed and took the bottle from Mallory. "Don't piss off the help, especially when it's free labor."

Grace just smiled and gave her a curious look.

Mallory winced. She'd have to watch her tone. "Well, I'd better get back to work."

Elaine was garnishing the drinks Gunner had made and grinning at something he said. Mallory spotted two tickets with beer orders and she slid in to man the tap.

"I can deliver these pitchers if you tell me which tables," she told Elaine, who'd been moving nonstop.

"Nah, I should be back by the time you're finished." She hefted the loaded tray and nodded toward the stage. "The mug is for Mike. I'm pretty sure he'd rather you take it to him," she said with a mischievous smile before heading for the back room.

Mallory sighed. What was it with Elaine and Sadie? Why were they trying to fix her up with him?

"Who's Mike?"

She looked at Gunner. For a few wonderful, blessed moments, she'd forgotten he was there. "A guy who did some carpentry work for me." Gunner turned his head and she saw that his hair was touching the collar of his blue polo shirt. He never let it go like that, not even when he was away working for long periods of time. But damn he looked good.

"The guy sitting alone to the left of the stage?" he asked, turning back to stare at her.

"What?"

"Is that Mike?"

"I don't know. I haven't looked for him. What do you care, anyway?" She noticed a couple sitting near Ben trying impatiently to get her attention. Damn. Her grand opening and she was going to chase everyone away.

She felt Gunner watching her as she went to get refills. Those mesmerizing gray eyes still got to her every time. When she'd first met him when she was sixteen, she hadn't been that into boys yet, but she remembered thinking he was the hottest guy she'd ever seen. He'd been twenty-one at the time so of course he'd barely noticed her.

For weeks he'd come to the bar almost every day. Then he'd disappear for a month. She'd known it was partly his job that kept him away. But when a year had gone by without him making a single appearance, she'd figured that was it…she'd never see him again. And then out of the blue Gunner had started showing up, three or four times a week when he wasn't away on location.

By then she'd turned twenty-one and was working full-time at the Renegade. A year later her dad had died unexpectedly. An aneurism, the doctor had said. No apparent cause. Mallory had figured all the hard living had caught up to him. Bitter that his stunt career had been cut short, he'd drank a lot, smoked anything that was rolled and screwed any woman who'd let him. He wasn't so different from a lot of the stunt guys who'd helped keep the Renegade in business.

Of course many just had one or two drinks then left to go home to their wives. Gunner fell somewhere in the middle. He'd done some hell-raising in his twenties but not lately. And while he could drink with the best of them, only twice had she seen him truly drunk.

Mallory slipped past him to get to the tap, and thankfully, Elaine returned at the same time. Questions burned in Gunner's eyes, but no way would Mallory deal with them now. Or ever, if she had her say.

"You didn't take Mike his beer," Elaine said, and then briefly eyed Gunner as if she'd just realized he might be the reason. "Never mind. I'll go."

Mallory watched her pick up the mug. She should've just taken it to Mike and thanked him for coming to the opening. But she couldn't do it in front of Gunner. It was stupid. But somehow she knew she'd fumble.

She felt those stormy gray eyes on her again. She turned and met them full-on. "What?"

He gave a slight shrug before looking to see if Elaine had left a ticket. She hadn't. It was the first lull of the night. He picked up a dry bar rag and wiped his hands.

"You need a haircut."

"I was too busy leaving voice mails."

Drawing in a deep breath, she avoided his gaze by checking the bowl of lime wedges. They still had a lot. She looked up and saw Mike lifting a hand. She smiled back at him.

Two tables to his left, she noticed a young woman who'd applied for the waitress job. Mallory couldn't recall her name, but Elaine would know. If the woman was willing, Mallory would hire her on the spot.

Either way, there was no need for Gunner to stay.

She was about to tell him so when she felt pressure around her waist.

It was Gunner.

Behind her. His hands sliding down to cup her hips.

"Excuse me, sweetheart," he said, trying, though not very hard, to move her to the right. "I need to get more glasses."

Without making a fuss, she managed to push his hands away. "Touch me again and I'll—" Okay, that might've been too loud. She clamped her lips together.

"What? Hmm, Mallory?" he whispered with a half smile. "What are you going to do? Move to Alaska?"

3

GUNNER KNEW HE shouldn't have come tonight. It was a dick move. Yeah, he was still pissed at Mallory. But he didn't want to screw things up for her. She probably already had first-night jitters.

"Excuse me," she said through gritted teeth and forced him back a step at the risk of losing his toes.

Those were some heels on her black boots. They looked new. And kind of sexy. Normally she wore a low-heeled tan pair that were pretty beat-up. And the clingy red top and tight black jeans? He'd never seen them before. At the Renegade she'd worn nothing but T-shirts and faded denim. And sometimes a flannel shirt in the winter.

The guys sitting at the bar all watched her walk to the other end, their gazes lingering on her ass before taking in her long legs. It annoyed the shit out of him.

On second thought, why should he worry about making her nervous? She'd done this to herself. All she'd had to do was return just one damn call. They could've talked, got everything out in the open. Not that he thought there was anything to hash out. The world hadn't ended just because they'd had sex.

And he sure as hell didn't remember holding a gun to her head. Mallory hadn't held back. Sure, the booze played a part, but they hadn't drank *that* much. He'd done a lot of thinking on the drive to Montana. Mallory had downed three quick shots in a row, but the tequila hadn't had time to kick in before they'd started kissing.

Okay, maybe she'd needed the liquid courage. If so, it sure had worked. She'd moaned so loud when she came he was surprised she hadn't set off the neighborhood dogs.

Gunner watched her lean over the bar and gesture to something in the back. With her bent at that angle, the guys were more interested in looking down her V-neck top than what she was pointing at.

He had to turn away. His insides were churning and he didn't trust himself to stay cool. If he caused a commotion, she'd never forgive him.

With more elbow grease than was necessary, he finished cleaning up his mess and let the sink fill with hot sudsy water while he poured himself a beer. Damn, he wanted something stronger. That would have to wait. After she closed, maybe they could sit down like two adults and figure this thing out.

"We have a dishwasher," Elaine said, setting down her tray and watching him lower glasses into the steaming sink.

"It's too small for this crowd. It'll be okay for normal nights."

"Obviously you're a friend of Mallory's," the petite brunette said. "I'm guessing you're from LA, but you're not a bartender."

"You got customers complaining about the drinks?"

"I should've said you don't look like one." Her gaze roamed his shoulders, his chest, then down to his boots. "With that tan, you must spend a lot of time outdoors. And you sure didn't get those arms from pouring whiskey. You could be a cowboy, I suppose, but I don't think so." She met his eyes and laughed. "Honey, I've got a husband and two teenagers. I took this job to get away from them, but I still love all three of 'em to death. So don't you worry, I'm just nosy."

Gunner dried his hands and took another pull of his beer. "There's a tanning salon at the gym where I work out."

Elaine's frown eased to a grin. "You're just piling it on, aren't you?"

He glanced over to see what was keeping Mallory. "Now, why would I do that?"

"Wait. You came in with Ben, so I'll bet you're a stuntman out there in California."

"That's one possibility."

"Although…" Elaine squinted at him as if the right guess came with a thousand-dollar prize. "It sounds like you got a trace of Texas in your voice."

Bullshit.

Gunner plunged his hands into the sudsy water—the very hot sudsy water—and bit back a curse. Hell, he'd left home at fifteen and wanted nothing to do with Texas. The dirty stinking town where he grew up was only half the size of Blackfoot Falls. So if your mom was the town tramp, everybody knew it.

A customer called for Elaine and she picked up her tray. "You'd better be nice to me," she said, grinning.

"I'm the only person standing between you and your fan club over there."

He didn't have to look to know which table she meant. The three women were from San Diego and staying at the Sundance Ranch. They'd been driving him nuts. He didn't go for the hair-twirling, lip-licking crap.

That was one great thing about Mallory. She didn't play games or work at being sexy. Of course with those big green eyes, generous mouth and killer body she didn't have to do anything.

So why the new clothes? She had no business looking hot as hell. Was this her turning over a new leaf? Making a fresh start? Had she been trying to get away from him? All she'd had to do was tell him to get lost.

One of the Sundance women had a thing for Blake Shelton, and had "Honey Bee" on repeat. Once he got the glasses washed he was gonna unplug that damn jukebox.

"It seems we've died down a bit." Mallory's voice startled him. "There's no reason for you to stick around. Go be with Ben and Grace."

He drained his beer and looked at her. She was close. A couple feet away, her eyes full of uncertainty. "You look nice."

"Thanks." Her gaze flickered and lowered. "So do you."

"We have to talk."

"Please, Gunner. Not here. Please."

"You don't return my calls."

"I know. But I was busy getting moved out of the Renegade and then—" She shook her head, looked away. "You're right. I have no excuse. I should've talked to you."

"Damn right you should have." He was getting worked

up again, seeing her hang her head like a whipped dog. Looking as if he'd treated her badly. She was in the wrong, not him.

"Pardon me, but could I get another rum and Coke?"

Gunner recognized the husky voice before he glanced at the flirty redhead. "Just a minute," he said and turned back to Mallory.

She stared back at him for a second and then rolled her eyes. "Is that with a lime?" she asked the woman and grabbed the rum.

"Yes, lime, a wedge on the rim and another squeezed in the drink. And no offense, but I really like the way he makes it."

Mallory darted him a look, the expression on her face not one he'd seen before. When she finally smiled, it didn't fool him. She seemed sad, and he didn't understand why.

To get rid of the redhead, he stepped in and made her drink. Mallory turned and before she could walk away, he said, "Hey, don't run off."

She just glanced at him as she bent to check the dishwasher. He slid the rum and Coke toward the woman and went to Mallory. He almost reached for her hand, but thought better of it. Part of him wanted to comfort her, the other part was having trouble controlling his temper.

"Why?" he asked, careful to keep his voice low. "Just tell me why."

"Gunner..." Her head down, she opened the dishwasher. Steam poured out. He caught her arm to pull her away just as she jerked back.

"Are you okay?"

She nodded. "I thought the heat cycle was finished."

"Let me see," he said, brushing the hair away from her face.

"I'm fine." The warning tone in her voice was enough. She didn't have to flinch from his touch.

Anger flared inside him, and then simmered to concern when he noticed the red blotch. "You have a small burn," he said, nodding at her chin.

Her hand shot to her cheek.

"Closer to your—" Screw it. He directed her unsteady fingers to the spot. "Where's the first-aid kit?" The one she'd kept at the Renegade had been put to good use.

"I don't know. I'm still unpacking stuff."

"I saw a store on the way here. I'll go—"

Mallory shook her head. "Everything is closed by now." She probed around the reddened skin. "It doesn't feel bad. I'll be okay." Turning toward Ben and Grace, she gave them a self-conscious smile. Then she looked at Gunner again and the soft expression in her eyes told him right then and there he'd done the right thing by coming to Montana. "You didn't tell them, did you?"

"Tell them?" His confusion took a second to clear. "Christ, give me some credit." Shaking his head, he picked up the pile of tip money people had left him and stuffed it in Elaine's jar on the back shelf.

"Where are you going?" Mallory almost sounded like she cared.

He knew better. "To find a friendlier bar," he said, and almost plowed into Elaine as he headed for the door.

GUNNER HAD JUST finished his first shot of tequila when Ben entered the Watering Hole. Figured he hadn't been far behind. The place was dead except for a pair of pool players in the back and a table of old-timers laughing at each other's lame jokes. He wished they'd keep it down.

"Hey, Nikki," Ben said as he took the barstool next to Gunner.

The pretty, dark-haired bartender stopped restocking the fridge and turned. "Hey yourself," she said. "What can I get you?"

Gunner pushed his empty shot glass toward her.

"Beer for me," Ben said, and inclined his head at Gunner. "He's buying."

"Sure." Gunner snorted. "Why not? In fact, pour something for yourself, darlin', and put it on my tab."

Nikki glanced at him, smiled at Ben, then got his beer and Gunner's shot.

"You might as well leave the bottle," Gunner said when she turned to put the tequila back on the shelf.

"Nope. I don't do that." She leaned a hip against the back bar. "How's Mallory holding up?"

Gunner grunted and tossed back the liquor. He felt Ben staring at him. Of course he was going to have questions. And Gunner had no idea what to tell him.

"She's doing all right, considering she should've had two more waitresses working," Ben said. "Gunner was helping make drinks until a few minutes ago."

The bartender gave him a curious look. "I'm Nikki McAllister," she said, leaning forward and shaking hands with him.

"Gunner." He saw a gold wedding band on her finger.

Not that he was interested. A few months ago…yeah, he might've been looking to hook up. But things had shifted for him around Christmas…about the time something had changed between him and Mallory.

He couldn't say what exactly, or why he'd suddenly

noticed how her smile lit up a room. Even her laugh sounded different now. And there was something about the way she looked at him. It gave him the weirdest feeling inside...

Shit.

It was for the best she'd moved away. He didn't need this grief. He'd liked his life just the way it was before. Thirty-two was too young for a midlife crisis. He'd find a new bar, or just follow the rest of the gang. Guaranteed they'd already adopted some dive that served cheap drinks.

Was that what he really wanted? Nothing felt right. He wasn't into the job anymore. It had gotten so that he hated traveling.

He'd been staring at his empty shot glass for a while. When he looked up, Nikki wasn't behind the bar. And Ben had actually shifted on his stool to face him.

"What the hell is going on with you?" Ben asked. "You've been distracted and edgy since you got here."

Gunner sighed. He'd met Ben while they were filming in Mexico years ago. They'd become casual friends. Or at least they'd built enough trust between them to watch each other's backs. "Just tired. Argentina was a bitch even before we fell behind schedule."

"Yeah, I always hated those long stretches. Ranching has been an adjustment. Hell, I'm up well before dawn every morning. But I don't miss it."

Gunner leaned back to ease the kink from two days of hard driving. "I wondered if you had any regrets."

"Nope." Ben shook his head. "They've been filming around Glacier National Park and south along the Rockies. I picked up some work after I first bought the ranch. I had to sink a bundle into repairs and stock, so it made sense to bring in a little cash and keep my union benefits. But I've decided I'm done with stunt work," he said, shrugging. "You know, I've got Grace now. I don't like being away from her."

Gunner never thought he'd hear those words come out of Ben Wolf's mouth. Not that long ago Ben had had quite a reputation for going through women like he went through booze, fancy cars and speeding tickets.

"You still have a driver's license?" Gunner asked.

"Yeah," Ben said with a grin. "You?"

"Yep. How's your record here? Any tickets yet?"

"How do you think I met Grace?"

Right. She was the sheriff. "She wrote you up? You couldn't sweet-talk her out of it?"

Ben didn't answer. Just smiled and lifted his mug.

Letting out a laugh, Gunner clapped him on the back. "Dude, you got it bad."

Ben eyed him with raised brows.

Gunner was pretty sure he knew what was coming next. Couldn't say he hadn't asked for it. Though he didn't think he'd been too obvious with Mallory.

Glancing around, he searched for Nikki, who was probably in the back. The tequila shots hadn't done a damn thing for him. Which was just as well. Unless he wanted to end up sleeping it off in his truck, he needed to pay up and get out of here.

Ben nodded at the empty shot glass. "Might want to ease up since we drove separately."

"Sure, Dad."

"Suit yourself. But if you get stopped by a deputy, don't expect Grace to cut you a break." Ben pushed his unfinished beer away and stood. "Tomorrow I'll show you around the Silver Spur. The place still needs work and I might've gotten ahead of myself drumming up business." He turned to go but then paused. "We leave the kitchen door unlocked. You remember how to get back?"

Gunner nodded.

"Drive carefully," he said as he headed for the door. "Lots of deer are on the roads after dark."

Drive carefully.

Yep, Ben had changed.

Gunner tried to remember how long it had been since Ben had left Hollywood. Over a year for sure, but not all that long considering how well he'd settled into his quiet new life.

Like Ben had said, part of it was Grace. Gunner had hauled ass from California to make it in time for Mallory's opening night. So he'd only met Grace an hour before the three of them had come to town. But he'd liked her right off. She seemed to be straightforward, had a good sense of humor and a street-smart air about her. And she was pretty.

Come to think of it, she reminded him of Mallory.

So if Ben and Grace could make a go of it...

There was a big difference. Ben and Grace didn't share any history. The only things she knew about Ben was what he'd told her. Mallory knew everything about Gunner, warts and all as the saying went. And he had some pretty damn ugly warts in his past.

4

MALLORY KICKED AN empty box to the side and studied the stack she hadn't opened yet. Most of them were marked by room, but where the rest belonged was anyone's guess. At least she had plenty of space in the two-bedroom rental. Yes, she supposed it was small by most standards, but to her it was a palace. She'd never lived in a house before.

Not only that but the rent was crazy cheap. Way lower than she'd been prepared to pay. And talk about convenient…she was just off Main, an eight-minute walk from the bar. Six, if she was in a hurry.

Gunner wasn't going to believe—

She stopped the thought cold.

Things were different now. She wouldn't be telling Gunner about every stupid little thing that happened in her day. In her life. When had they started doing that anyway? Hanging out at the Renegade on slow nights, huddled at the end of the bar, just the two of them, talking about nothing? Sometimes, shooting pool in the back and making crazy bets. Or calling each other at odd times just to let off steam?

She'd never had a real friend before Gunner. Not even in high school because the girls her age had only wanted to talk about boys and clothes. Although it was just in the past two years that she and Gunner had started to test the waters, throwing out tidbits of personal stuff. Nothing big, but she was going to miss all of that.

She was going to miss *him*.

Dammit.

Why had he shown up here? Seeing him last night was like ripping off a scab before the wound had healed. Of course she was to blame. She should've answered his calls. Pretended the best she could that nothing had changed. Then done the only thing that had a chance of solving her problem…moving as far away from him as possible. With the expired lease and ridiculous rent hike she'd had the perfect excuse to relocate.

Instead she'd shut him out and ran. Out of fear. Out of embarrassment. But most of all, she'd fled for self-preservation. None of it mattered now. She would have to face him and explain why she'd behaved like the silly school girls she hadn't wanted as friends.

Well, no, not exactly. Mallory knew an explanation was unavoidable, but she was perfectly willing to play fast and loose with the truth. She'd have to be an utter moron to admit that she'd gone and done the stupidest thing ever.

She'd developed *feelings* for Gunner.

Her friend.

The guy who would hotfoot it all the way to the moon rather than be tied down to any one woman. Let alone her. Someone he expected to know better than to mistake sex for anything but sex.

And if that wasn't enough to make her want to disappear from the face of the earth, jealousy had her by the throat. *Her.* She was supposed to be immune to that sort of pettiness.

Oh, she'd guessed after that night she might have a problem with the way women threw themselves at him. It was another reason she'd run. But watching how women had reacted to him last night was so much worse than she'd imagined.

She drew in a deep breath and glanced around. She had a lot to do. Her new living room was narrow but clean and rustic, and she loved having a fireplace. She didn't even mind that it took up a third of the brick wall. But it was the wraparound porch with a perfect view of the Rockies that had stolen her heart. The owners had even left a swing and a wooden rocking chair. If she didn't have so much unpacking to do, she'd be out there right now, lounging on the swing and sipping an iced tea.

Boy, that was a hard image to picture. Much too homey and so not her.

She would never let Gunner see the place. For sure he'd think she'd lost it. The possibility wasn't too far out there. What else would explain her decision to start moving in now? She was paid up at The Boarding House Inn for two more days and she was still wiped out from last night. If she believed Sadie, and it seemed the woman was never wrong, the Full Moon would be packed tonight again.

Luckily, Mallory had a woman wanting part-time work coming in later to talk to her. Elaine had vouched for her. It would simply be a matter of agreeing on schedules.

She ripped the tape off a box and then heard her phone. It wasn't in her pocket. She listened, thought the ring might be coming from the kitchen. By the time she found her cell under a pile of newspapers, the caller had been sent to voice mail. But she recognized Dexter's number and saw that he'd also called forty minutes ago.

Mallory listened carefully to his awkward message and sighed. She disconnected and looked at the time. If she'd understood correctly, he'd be delivering the bull in about ten minutes.

Great. She had no one to help her unload and set up. Damn, she couldn't even call Ben now that Gunner was staying at the Silver Spur. Hopefully, Dexter was bringing someone with him.

She made it to the bar just as a pair of brawny cowboys climbed out of an old blue truck parked at the curb.

"Mornin'," the taller man said, touching the brim of his hat. "We heard you might need some help?"

"Yes, but how would— Sadie?"

He grinned and nodded. "I'm Brady. This here is Tom."

"Pleased to meet you, ma'am," Tom said and yanked off his cowboy hat, revealing a buzz cut.

"I'm Mallory." She stepped forward and shook their hands. Both men were about her age, she guessed, and looked nice and strong. "I appreciate this so much. Of course I'll pay you for—"

"No, ma'am. We volunteered." Tom seemed offended.

"It's our day off." Brady lifted his hat and swept back his longish blond hair before resetting the hat on his head. He was kind of cute. Great smile. And he seemed familiar. "We're on our own time and just wanna help."

"Oh, well…" She studied him more closely. "You were here at the opening last night. Sitting near the jukebox…" She took a guess. "Both of you…"

They nodded, clearly pleased she remembered them. "We're real glad you opened the place," Brady said. "The Watering Hole is okay but it gets old."

The sound of a sputtering engine had her glancing over her shoulder. "I think this might be Dexter," she said, shading her eyes and watching the ancient pickup slow down. "Look, guys, if you won't let me pay you then I'm giving you free drinks for a week. Sound fair?"

"No need—" Brady protested.

"Good. It's settled." She dug a key out of her jeans pocket and unlocked the door to the bar.

The bull was a monstrosity. It sat in the bed of the truck covered by a white tarp. After a word with Dexter, she hurried inside to clear a path to the back room. Brady followed behind her, picking up the solid oak tables as if they weighed nothing.

Tom joined them and the two men scoped out the spot for the bull and strategized the best way to bring it inside. They didn't ask for her opinion, in fact they mostly ignored her. And as they maneuvered the bull through the double doors and she tried to help, she was politely ordered to stay out of the way.

Mallory wasn't used to being dismissed. Nor had she ever been comfortable with depending on anyone, much less strangers, to do things for her. She'd always hated asking for help, even as a kid. Luckily she was generally self-sufficient.

Moving back to give them a wide path into the back room, she told herself this was a different culture out here. They hadn't really dismissed her. But it was still hard not to jump into the mix as she watched these young husky guys labor under the weight of the bull. Surely it would be better with three people...

Tom momentarily lost his footing, and she stepped forward.

"Don't do it, Mallory."

At the sound of Gunner's voice, she started to turn around. But his hands cupped her shoulders and he drew her several steps backward, until she came up against his chest.

She jerked free and glared at him. "Don't do what?"

"Get in their way," he said, his gaze trained on the men. "You're liable to get someone hurt."

Even though they were no longer touching, she could feel the tension in his body. Nothing showed in his face as he sidestepped her and whipped off his black Stetson. Her favorite.

"Hey, guys, let me give you a hand." He pressed the hat to her and she hugged it to her chest.

"We got it," Brady said, but they were obviously struggling.

Gunner grabbed hold and they managed to carry the bull to the padding she'd had installed in the wood floor. She fought the urge to point out the bull belonged in the reinforced center, afraid they might tear the padding. She figured Gunner had already noticed and would make allowances.

"Ready to set her down?" Gunner asked.

"Ready," Tom said.

Brady didn't answer.

"Let's try to avoid the padded area," Gunner said mildly. "Now, on the count of three. One…two…three."

The bull landed dead center.

Sighing with relief, she loosened her death grip on his hat.

Tom stumbled back a step, and then let out a winded

laugh. "The sucker is heavy." He nodded at Gunner. "Thanks."

"We were doing just fine," Brady said, wiping the sweat from his forehead with the back of his arm. "You didn't need to jump in."

Tom shook his head. "I'm shorter than you so I was having trouble with the angle."

"It's done. That's what's important, right?" Gunner clapped Brady on the back. "Now, what can I get you boys? How about a nice cold beer?"

Mallory saw the startled look that passed between the two cowboys, and she wanted to give Gunner a swift kick in his rear. He had no business acting like he owned her and the bar.

"Sure," she said with a bright smile. "Help yourselves to whatever you want while I go pay Dexter." She paused. "I'm sorry for not introducing you to Gunner." She widened her smile and tossed him his hat. "My *cousin* is visiting for a little while."

"Oh." Brady grinned and shook his hand. "I saw you last night. You just get in yesterday?"

Gunner started to laugh, a loud belly laugh that followed her out to the sidewalk. He wanted to talk? Oh yeah, they were going to have a conversation all right. The second she saw Dexter leaning against his truck, hands stuffed in his baggy overalls, his eyelids drooping under a battered straw hat, she remembered something.

He straightened when he saw her, his mouth lifting in a gap-toothed grin. "They get Fanny in there okay?"

"Yes, they did." She passed him the envelope. "Cash. Just like you wanted."

"Well, I reckon I don't need to count it, do I?"

"I'm pretty good at math. It's all there." She smiled. "Now, how about that demo?"

Frowning, he pushed up the rim of his hat. "What's that?"

"You know, show me how to work it."

"Oh, good thing you said something." He opened the driver's door and brought out a short stack of papers, the top right corners curled up from what looked like a dried coffee stain. She hoped. Chewing tobacco seemed to be a favorite pastime with some of the men around town. It was gross.

"This here is the manual," Dexter said, holding the papers out to her. "Tells you everything you need to know."

Oh, God, there were a lot more stains. She forced herself to accept it. "Thank you," she said. "This will help. But I'd really like you to show me—"

"You mean get up there and ride Fanny?" He snorted a laugh. "Nooo. That's not gonna happen. I don't recall agreeing to anything of the kind."

Mallory rubbed her right temple. Yes, he most certainly had agreed, in fact he'd offered.

"Tell you what... I'll stick around until you get her plugged in and working." He closed the door. "Help ease your mind some."

"Thank you," she said and led him into the Full Moon.

A bark of laughter greeted them. As they neared the back room, she heard the whir of a motor and a fair amount of squeaking. Something sure needed to be oiled.

Of course it was Gunner sitting on top of the bull, holding on with one hand while it bucked and whirled. Brady watched from the sidelines drinking from a long-neck, while Tom had the controls that tempered the speed and buck of the bull. Both cowboys were grinning like kids.

"Can't that thing go faster?" Brady asked, nudging Tom with an elbow to the ribs.

"You're welcome to get up here and see for yourself," Gunner said, his black T-shirt stretching across his broad shoulders.

Mallory stared at his chest and stomach. He wasn't moving much, just holding on to the short leather strap, his other hand in the air for balance. But her gaze was caught by the way the muscles in his arms and thighs rippled with even the tiniest movement.

Brady set down his beer. "I've ridden my share of ornery broncs," he said, and flexed his shoulders and arms. "I can handle a piece of machinery."

"Better you get thrown now than in front of those gals from the Sundance," Tom said, chuckling.

"Well, heck, he makes it look too dang easy." Watching Gunner, Dexter removed his straw hat and scratched his head.

Mallory waved to get Gunner's attention. "Would you please turn that off for a minute?"

He nodded at Tom, and with a fluid grace that always made her breath catch, Gunner landed on his feet.

She made a quick introduction. "Can you think of anything we need to ask Dexter before he leaves?"

Gunner turned to eye the bull, showing no reaction to the error she'd made by using *we*. "I would've thought you'd have oiled that thing up before bringing it."

"Well, son, I surely did just that." Dexter sounded defensive.

"Okay. I believe you." Gunner nodded. "But that tells me we've got a problem. Whatever is causing the squeaking is gonna need more work than a simple servicing."

Mallory hadn't thought of that.

Dexter's face turned red. "I reckon you got a point."

"I take care of all the trucks and equipment at the Bar T," Brady said. "Can't promise I'll know what's wrong but I can have a look if you want."

He'd addressed Gunner, not Mallory, which irked her to no end. Aware she was partly to blame, she kept her cool and just listened to the men discuss what needed to be done. She liked to think she was independent, perfectly capable of running her own business, and mostly she did a good job. But for the past year she'd relied on Gunner for so many little things.

Once he'd given her a ride when her car was in the shop. Another time she'd asked his advice on whether or not to add a second pool table at the Renegade. Just minor things, but she couldn't deny she'd established a pattern.

She realized she'd blanked out of the conversation when she saw Gunner and Dexter shake hands. The older man gave her a polite nod and left.

"I assume that's okay with you," Gunner said, the amusement in his eyes making it clear he knew she'd zoned out.

"Of course, or I would've said something." She turned to Brady. "Will you have time to look at it soon? I'll pay you whatever you think is fair."

The look Brady and Tom exchanged told her that was the part she'd missed.

Gunner turned to the two men. "You guys can take off. I've got it from here."

Brady frowned. "Sadie thought you might need some

help moving into your new place," he said to Mallory. "Tom and I planned on giving you a hand."

"That's really nice." Mallory was genuinely touched and sorely tempted to accept their offer. Giving them each a smile, she shook her head. "I wouldn't feel right ruining your day off. You still get free drinks, though, so don't forget," she said and started herding them toward the door.

Brady seemed hesitant, glancing at Gunner, who hadn't moved. "It's really no trouble."

"Well, come on." She motioned for Gunner. "I'm locking up."

"Good." He folded his arms across his chest. "We need to talk."

5

GUNNER WOULDN'T HAVE been shocked if Mallory had run like hell once she got to the door and let the two men out. When she turned to him, the fear and dread he saw in her face twisted him up inside. This wasn't like her, running from a problem, not tackling it head-on.

"You want anything?" she asked as she slipped behind the bar and brought out a glass.

He used silence to get her to look up. "An explanation would be nice."

She blinked and focused on fixing herself a soda water with lime. "I was wrong for not returning your calls. I'm sorry."

Gunner waited, taking in the shadows under her eyes. She hadn't been sleeping well. Tough. Neither had he. "That's it?"

"I've been busy with the move."

"Ah, of course. I hadn't thought of that."

"Really?" Her chin came up. "Sarcasm?"

"Hey, whatever it takes to get you to open up." He held her gaze, watching the fire flash and die in her eyes. It was hard to watch this strong, fierce woman look away in defeat. Maybe he needed to let this go. For both their sakes. "You put me through hell the past five weeks. I want to know why."

"I didn't mean to," she said, her expression sad. "I thought the separation might do us some good—"

"Why?"

Her eyes narrowed. "I think you know why."

"We had sex, Mallory. Lots of friends do. It didn't mean anything." Gunner thought he saw her flinch. He could've phrased that better. "Okay, maybe it was stupid. You were worried about losing the Renegade. I was worried about you... We were both a little drunk. Are we going to let a brief lapse in judgment ruin our friendship?"

She stared down at her soda. "Well, we can't very well undo it, can we?"

"No, but we can move past—" A sickening thought occurred to him, one he hadn't considered before now. "Do you think I took advantage of you?"

Her eyes widened. "No."

"I didn't think you were that drunk."

"I wasn't... I—" She sighed. "That never even crossed my mind. Jesus. It goes both ways. Do you think I took advantage of *you*?"

Gunner chuckled. "Yeah, and I hated every minute of it."

She didn't crack a smile. Just muttered a curse when she spilled some soda.

"We can't fix this if you won't talk to me," he said, watching her scrub the bar as if her life depended on stripping off the varnish.

"Talk? You'd rather go to the ER."

Not completely true. He'd told her a few things he

hadn't admitted to anyone else. "This is different," he said, and she finally looked at him again. "Our friendship is on the line."

A slight smile lifted the corners of her lips. "I live here now. You'll find another bar in Valencia or Hollywood. This thing between us—this friendship—is bound to fizzle out. You know that as well as I do."

Gunner felt as if she'd stuck a knife in his chest. Guess he sucked at being a friend because that's not how he saw it. "Yep. You're right." He glanced at his watch. He was supposed to meet Ben in two hours.

"I was embarrassed," Mallory said softly. "That's why I stopped returning your calls." She'd quit attacking the varnish but she still had trouble meeting his eyes.

"Embarrassed? With me?"

"Yes you," she said, slowly shaking her head. "Especially you. Of all the guys I could've…" Pressing her lips together, she looked away.

"Go on," Gunner said. "Could've what?"

"Messed up with."

He didn't get it. "Look, if you're waiting for me to say I regret what happened, you can forget it. We had sex…pretty damn great sex as I recall." He watched her nibble her lower lip and his body tensed. "The truth is, I wanted you," he said. "I still want you."

Mallory's mouth opened and closed without her making a sound. She just stared at him, and damned if he could tell what she was thinking.

"But if you feel sex and friendship can't mix, then…" He cleared his throat. "We'll stay friends, while I lick my wounds in private."

She smiled.

"I'm glad my suffering can bring you some amusement."

"Ah. Poor Gunner." She dropped the towel on the bar and walked around to join him.

His heart started pounding...until she strolled right past him. He turned to see where she was going and noticed a guy peering in the window and pointing to the door. Mallory opened it just enough to tell him to come back at six.

Seeing her in her old jeans with the tear just above her right knee filled Gunner with an odd sort of relief. "No daytime hours?"

"Not for now. Maybe later, but only on weekends. I'll check with Sadie to see what she thinks. She used to open at four before she became mayor."

Just as Mallory was about to slip behind the bar, he caught her arm.

She stared at his hand, then into his eyes.

"Friends, right?"

"Yes." She nodded warily. "Friends."

"With or without sex?"

She just sighed and looked at him as if he had the attention span of a five-year-old.

Gunner smiled. "Okay," he said, releasing her arm and offering his hand. "No sex."

Her suspicious look might've been insulting if it hadn't been warranted. The second she grasped his hand he tugged her into his arms. He felt her stiffen when he brushed a kiss across her mouth. A second later she relaxed and moved her hands to his shoulders, then slid her fingers into his hair.

She felt so good against him, warm and soft and real. He'd imagined this every night he'd been stuck in Argentina. Every night except one. After the sixth day of unreturned calls, he'd gotten stinking drunk and blotted out the world. And paid for it the next day.

Mallory stirred in his arms and parted her lips. Their tongues touched. A soft helpless moan came from the back of her throat, lighting a fire in his belly that tested his self-control.

Mallory moved against him. All her sweet womanly curves hit him in all the right places. If he got any harder he was going to explode.

A firm shove to the chest sent him back a step. He lowered his arms to his side and met her dark green eyes.

"What's wrong with you?" She glared back. "We just agreed to be friends, no sex."

"Kissing isn't sex."

She was breathing hard, her breasts rising and falling. Gunner tried not to stare. Or think about the velvety texture of her skin. Or how sweet she'd tasted.

God, he wanted her.

"Mallory…"

"Don't say another word." She patted her pockets, glanced around until she found her keys behind the bar. "You need to leave. I have things to do."

"I can help you move."

"No." She rushed past him and unlocked the door. "Thank you."

Trust him to ruin things. He grabbed his Stetson off the bar and set it on his head. "Have I totally screwed up?"

With a warning glare, she held the door open. "No. But you probably should leave before you do."

"Copy that," he said, and walked out without looking back.

GUNNER HAD ARRIVED late yesterday afternoon and hadn't seen much of Ben's ranch yet. But it was clear a lot of hard work had gone into the Silver Spur even before Gunner had gotten the lowdown from the kid hired to help feed and water the animals and do odd jobs.

While Ben wrapped up a business call, Gunner waited outside the small barn office and talked to the boy. Billy, with his friendly face and jug ears, looked to be about seventeen and took pride in his work. Bales of hay were stacked in two corners, an entire wall of orderly tack looked well-maintained and he'd been cleaning saddles while he described the poor condition of the ranch before Ben had bought it.

"Sorry to keep you waiting." Ben closed the office door behind him.

Gunner saw the frustration in his face. "If this is a bad time I can get lost for a while."

"No. Now's good." Ben plowed a hand through his long dark hair and tugged on his hat. "Man, I hate turning down business."

"Better than burning yourself out or doing a half-assed job. You don't need that kind of rep in Hollywood."

"True." Ben glanced at the boy. "I might be out of service for a while. We're heading to the north pasture."

Billy jumped to his feet and almost tripped over his stool. "You want me to saddle the horses?"

Ben hesitated. "Sure. But take your time. I'm showing Gunner around here first."

Gunner followed Ben's lead and moved to the barn's entrance. Staying out of the blazing sun, they watched the long, lanky kid head for the stables.

"He seems like a good worker."

"Yep." Ben nodded. "But a little accident-prone. I

know it kills him that I don't let him work with the horses."

"Maybe he'll grow out of it." Gunner shrugged. "I was on the clumsy side in my teens."

Ben eyed him. "You serious?"

"And hungry enough to get over it."

With a faint smile, Ben nodded. He'd also lived on the streets as a kid and understood what it took to get enough food in your belly. In order to survive, Gunner had learned how to steal and not get caught. Making restitution later had helped, but he hated remembering those bleak days.

Ben turned and glanced around the inside of the barn. "The loft has been reinforced. And I had the worse half of the roof repaired but the whole thing needs new shingles. That's coming from the walls," he said, gesturing to the cracks of sunlight that streaked the shadows. "I'm still working on that, but so far it's stayed fairly dry in here."

"I'm pretty good with a hammer," Gunner said. "I can work on it tomorrow."

"I thought you'd be helping Mallory move into her new place."

"Who told you that?"

"Grace." Ben laughed. "Who else?"

"Well, then she knows more than I do."

"Grace saw her parking the U-Haul in front of the house she rented. It's just off Main." Ben frowned. "Grace offered our help, but Mallory said she had it covered. I figured that was you."

"I saw her at the bar earlier," Gunner said evenly, hoping Ben wouldn't ask any questions. "She had something going on so we're supposed to talk later."

"I meant to ask, how long are you staying?"

"A week. Ten days maybe." It had a lot to do with Mallory. "Unless you kick me out sooner."

"Not if you're fixing my barn, I won't."

Gunner smiled and moved toward the entrance. "The stable looks new."

"It is. That's where I've sunk the most money so far," Ben said as they walked out under the hot July sun. "The place was a steal but I knew it would take a lot of work. It came with some equipment, though again, none of it in great shape, but good enough to float me for a couple of years."

They passed the corrals, several of them obviously new, and stopped to look at a pair of fine-looking roans prancing restlessly and testing the rails. "You bought these two locally?"

Nodding, Ben propped his elbows on the railing and studied the horses. "From the McAllister family. They own the Sundance where I grew up."

"I thought the Sundance was a dude ranch."

Ben winced. "The McAllister brothers are cattlemen. Their sister, Rachel, set up a way to accommodate guests when the economy took a dive, but raising cattle is their mainstay. Trace, the youngest brother, likes breeding horses."

Gunner didn't know anything about Ben's childhood or why he'd ended up living rough in LA. They'd never had that kind of personal relationship. "You get along with them?"

"Oh yeah. Good guys. You'll like them. And Matt Gunderson, too. He's married to Rachel and owns the Lone Wolf Ranch. Talk about a sweet operation—"

"Gunderson? The bull rider? Won a couple of world titles?"

"That's him."

"Wasn't he ranked number one or two, then just kind of dropped out of the pro tour?"

"Yep. He's a stock contractor now. Jumped in with both feet and already he's raised a champion bull."

"Jesus, must be something in the water around here," Gunner said, and Ben gave him a puzzled look. "No disrespect to Blackfoot Falls, and you seem content, but I don't get it."

"Small towns make you itch?"

"You could say that."

"It's not so bad here." Ben pushed off the rail and they continued toward the stable. "Mallory seems to like it."

"She's only been here three weeks."

"True. Hell, I should've talked her into getting out of the bar business and partnering with me," Ben said with a laugh.

Gunner looked over at him, not sure if he'd been joking or not.

"The part I dislike the most is the traveling. It's not a lot but there's always going to be stock to deliver and pick up." Ben glanced back at the roans. "I'm taking those geldings fifty miles south where they're shooting a miniseries. In two months an indie is being shot nearby."

"Yeah? Whose film?"

"Jason Littleton. A new up-and-comer according to the location scout who was here earlier this month."

"I might have heard the name."

Up ahead Billy led two saddled horses out of the stable. And for the next hour Gunner and Ben rode the north pasture and the perimeter of the five-hundred-acre spread.

As Ben described his plans for the future, Gunner kept wondering if Ben really was looking for a partner. He had more business than he could handle and his enthusiasm sounded a lot like a sales pitch.

Sure, Gunner was getting tired of stunt work. But he wasn't ready to call it quits just yet. He had money saved, so that wasn't the issue. Small towns didn't agree with him. And then there was Mallory to consider. She claimed she'd been embarrassed. But he wasn't totally convinced she hadn't left California to get away from him.

6

"How about Sunday and Monday?" Sadie asked. "They're slow nights. And that would give you two days off in a row."

"It doesn't matter to me." Mallory was about to check the time on her cell phone when she heard someone knock.

Very annoying since she'd put up a sign that she'd open at six. She turned and saw it was Elaine and a woman Mallory had met briefly the day before.

"Is that Heather Andrews with Elaine?" Sadie asked, frowning at the blonde. "She looking for a job?"

Mallory stopped halfway to the door. She hadn't hired her yet and Sadie's tone indicated she thought Heather might not be a good choice. "Something I should know about her?"

"Not really. She and Trevor just got divorced and I heard she was moving to Boise."

Wow, did everyone know everyone else's business? Small-town living sure took a different mind-set, Mallory thought, and made it a few more steps before Sadie stopped her again.

"I should warn you, though. This is Heather's third split. It won't take her long to hitch her wagon again, so you might wanna keep an eye on that fine-looking man of yours."

Mallory laughed. "No worries there. He's not mine." She turned away from Sadie's curious expression and unlocked the door.

Mallory pasted on a smile but she could feel the bias toward the woman building inside her. Heather was exactly Gunner's type—tall, slim and blonde, big blue eyes and a sultry smile. She'd likely be a great waitress. Guys would keep drinking just to flirt with her.

And that included Gunner.

Maybe.

It didn't matter. Mallory's nerves would do her in either way as she waited, wondering if they'd hook up. And feeling tense and irritable right up to the moment Gunner left with Heather. Or any other woman. That was precisely the sort of nonsense Mallory had moved away from California to avoid. Because like it or not, she'd become infatuated with the man who'd had no problem admitting that their night of intimacy meant nothing to him.

We had sex, Mallory. It didn't mean anything.

Gunner's words had played in her head, over and over, like the worst earworm in the history of the world. The mindless task of unpacking boxes hadn't helped. Too much time to think. For heaven's sake, she'd known the sex meant nothing without him saying so.

It happened…it shouldn't have. She needed to get over it already.

Elaine strolled in first. "Wow, the place looks good.

Here I thought I'd finish the cleanup before we opened. Oh, and you remember Heather."

"Of course." Mallory held on to the smile.

"Hi," Heather said with a small wave, wearing denim cutoffs so short they had to be illegal in most states.

Elaine glanced back as Mallory was about to lock the door again. "You might wanna leave it. I saw Gunner just— Oh, here he is."

Mallory sucked in a breath. He was right there, looking at her through the window, clean-shaven, which was unusual, and his slicked-back hair looked damp. Dark glasses hid his eyes. When his mouth curved in a slow sexy smile, she lowered her gaze and opened the door. Much as she would've loved locking him out, it would only stir up everyone's curiosity.

"What are you doing here?" she asked casually.

"I figured I'd have a look at that bull. With any luck I'll get it working for tonight." Wearing soft worn jeans, scuffed tan boots and a white T-shirt, he walked past her, carrying a small toolbox.

"Did the mechanical bull get here?" Elaine asked excitedly, and hurried to the back room.

Heather didn't seem to give a crap about the bull. Or anything except Gunner.

"Well, I best be going and letting you get back to work." Sadie pushed to her feet. "We'll talk again soon. Think about what I said…" Her mischievous grin made it clear she was referring to Heather and not which nights to close.

Mallory couldn't help but smile as she watched Sadie slip out and then turned to see she'd been deserted. The other three were in the back room. So she took a moment to breathe, while reminding herself that petty jealousy was no reason not to hire someone. Besides, if she wanted the mechanical bull to be a full feature, she or Elaine had to be at the controls. Which meant without a third person working it could only run when things were slow.

"Heather? Aren't you here about the waitress job?"

"Oh, yes." Heather murmured something to Gunner and Elaine then joined Mallory.

Ten minutes later, the Full Moon officially had a third waitress. Heather agreed to cover Elaine's days off and then work as needed, starting with tonight. Sheila, the other woman Mallory had already hired, worked at the Watering Hole but would fill in two nights a week here. Employing part-timers still meant more paperwork for Mallory. At the Renegade she'd occasionally used college kids to help out...off the books. She'd never had real employees before.

And then of course Gunner had always jumped in. Even when she hadn't needed the help, come to think of it... He'd spent more time behind the bar with her than sitting on a stool drinking.

Leaving Heather to finish filling out paperwork, Mallory went to check on Gunner. She found him lying on his back tinkering with something under the metal beast. Elaine had just handed him a wrench and was eyeing his flat abs and bulging biceps.

When she finally pulled her gaze away to look at Mallory, Elaine grinned. "How about you take over so I can show Heather what's what?"

Gunner brought his head up just as she nodded.

"Oh, Elaine... I've decided to close on Sundays. Monday is still up in the air. I'll be thinking about it and we'll talk later."

"I'll still need Wednesdays off. I hope that's not a problem."

"Nope. I've already put Heather on the schedule."

"Thanks." Elaine swooped down to pick up a piece of torn napkin stuck to a chair leg and then continued on.

Mallory smiled. Lucky for her Sadie had recommended the woman. Eventually Elaine would be able to run the bar in Mallory's absence.

Aware Gunner was still watching her, she centered her attention on the bull. "So what do you think?"

"You never closed the Renegade. Only for those two days when your pop died."

"It's different here," she said, glancing at him because he sounded so shocked. "Anyway, I was asking about Fanny."

"Different how?"

"Um, just about everything. The type of customers. And counting the dance floor, this place is three times the size of the Renegade. I also have employees now, and paperwork. And who knows? Maybe I'll even have a life."

She hadn't meant to get carried away. Her voice had risen, though she didn't think the other two heard. Gunner regarded her with an impassive expression that drove her nuts. She really hated that he could shut off emotions at will. She'd seen him do it a thousand times. Sometimes she could read him. But not often.

"I have a question," he said.

She braced herself, nodded.

"Did you call this bull Fanny?"

At first she just stared at him, but the question was so unexpected she started laughing.

"Fanny," he murmured, shooting another look at the

bull, and then turning back to Mallory. "Do I need to explain the facts of life to you?"

That was another thing… Gunner could always make her laugh. Well, no, not always. Sometimes she wanted to rip him a new one. "Sure, go ahead. I'd like to hear your take."

Still lying on his back, he pushed away from the bull and glanced around. "You have a storage room or someplace private? I'd be happy to show you."

She let out a very unladylike snort. "You wish…"

"You have no idea," he said, and reached a hand out.

Mallory stared at it, reluctant to touch him. Finally she gave in and he sprung to his feet…without any help from her.

His palm was tough with calluses, his hand so much larger than hers, but he was careful not to squeeze too tight as he tugged her closer.

Just as he'd been so careful with her that earth-shattering night that now felt like eons go.

For as long as she lived she'd remember the hot, hungry look on his face when he'd bared her breasts. She wasn't sure why she'd expected him to rush to the finish, maybe even get a little rough once the clothes came off. Probably because Gunner was such a physical guy.

But he'd handled her so gently, as if she was something precious and fragile, it had brought tears to her eyes. Tears she'd refused to let him see, even as he learned every inch of her body with his sure tongue and light touch.

No one had ever treated her like that. Since she'd been a kid Mallory had had a reputation for being tough. She was Coop Brandt's daughter, people would say… *No*

need to worry about her...she comes from strong stock...
she can handle anything.

And with a single touch, Gunner had turned it all
into a lie.

She stood perfectly still, fighting a rush of longing,
the need for him so great she feared she would never be
able to control it.

Heat blazed in his darkened eyes. "I missed you,"
he whispered.

Too surprised to respond, Mallory swallowed. The
words got stuck in her throat. She glanced over her
shoulder to see if anyone was watching, then looked
into his face.

His faint smile faded. Releasing her, he plowed his
hand through his damp hair.

"Gunner..." Her voice wavered.

He shrugged and turned to the bull. "It's in decent
shape. Just needs a good lube job."

Her mind went exactly where it shouldn't and she
coughed to cover a small whimper. "You have stuff on
your shirt," she said, pointing to his back. "Obviously I
did a crappy job sweeping."

"What kind of stuff?" he asked, craning his neck
to see.

She dusted him off, the tempting feel of hard muscle
and warm skin beneath the thin material making her
stop abruptly. "You had to wear white?"

"You know me," Gunner said. "I have spares in the
truck." He glanced at her tightly clasped hands and finished brushing himself off. "Shouldn't take me long to
get—this thing ready for tonight."

"You mean Fanny?"

He shook his head. "You have to think up a new name."

"That's what Dexter called her. I thought it was weird at first but it's starting to grow on me."

"Do you have any idea how many guys will try to explain why you shouldn't call a bull Fanny?"

Mallory laughed. But yeah, that would be super annoying. "Maybe we'll start out with Fanny, then have a contest to see who comes up with the best name. Winner drinks free for two nights."

"You're the boss," he said, and started rifling through the toolbox.

"You don't have to fix it now. I need to read the manual and know what I'm doing before I let customers ride."

"I'm familiar with this model. I can handle that for you."

"I appreciate the offer," she said slowly. "I do. But what happens after you leave? It'll be just me."

His expression cooled, though she didn't know why. She hadn't meant anything. It was the truth.

"Hey, Mallory," Elaine called out. "I can't find the salt for the margaritas."

"Oh, crap." Mallory checked the time, afraid she'd have to make a dash to the Food Mart. Last night's run on margaritas had almost wiped them out of key ingredients. "Be right there."

"Those frozen drinks are going to kill you," Gunner said.

"I know. I'm seriously thinking of—"

"Telling them the blender is broken?"

Mallory laughed.

Gunner smiled.

They'd been doing that a lot in the past few months. Finishing each other's sentences. Exchanging private looks.

Damn him for coming to Blackfoot Falls. She'd had three weeks to get used to being here on her own. Three weeks that felt more like three years whenever thoughts of him had sneaked in. But she'd been making headway. And now she would have to start all over again.

"Here you go, handsome." Heather bent forward to set a frosty mug of beer in front of Gunner, deliberately giving him a clear view of the goods under her snug top.

Instead, he glanced at the mug he had yet to finish. "I didn't order another one."

"No, silly. It's from a secret admirer."

Business had started off with a bang the second Mallory had opened the door two hours ago. And yet she'd turned down his offer to help. So here he sat at a corner table, watching her and stewing. "Did Mallory send the beer?"

"Nope." Heather flashed him a big smile. "It's from me."

So much for the secret part. He pushed the mug back to her. "Thanks anyway."

"Really?" Her eyes widened. "You're not leaving, are you?"

"Not yet."

Judging by her baffled frown, he guessed she wasn't used to being turned down. He could see why. Great body. Pretty blue eyes. The blond hair was fake, though. He wasn't sure about the sizable rack. But he had no desire to find out.

She glanced over her shoulder. "I know you and Mallory are just friends so I'm not doing anything wrong."

"How do you know that?"

"She told me." Heather batted her lashes, thick from too much makeup. "Said I could have you all to myself."

"Did she?" He took a slow sip of beer. In his rotten mood he had to be careful. It would be easy to get drunk.

"Dammit, Heather." Face flushed, Elaine came up behind Heather. In between taking orders she'd been manning the tap. "You have three tables waiting for you."

"Okay already, tell them I'll be right there."

"Tell them yourself," Elaine grumbled and turned to go.

"Elaine?" Gunner had kept his gaze on Mallory but she hadn't looked over once. "I can take over the tap."

"God bless you," she said, using her shoulder to blot her damp face. "I'll even split my tips with you."

He smiled, dropped some money on Heather's tray and walked past her. Just as he slid behind the bar, Mallory looked up. "I told you I don't need your help."

"Elaine says you do." Putting his hands on her waist, he moved her over. Then took possession of the tap. She didn't bite his head off for touching her so that was progress.

"Fine. I do. What I don't need is you flirting with the waitresses or anyone else while you're working back here."

"Why?" He grinned. "You jealous?"

She glared. "I don't need a parade of women causing a bottleneck. Go back to your table and flirt all you want."

"I'm not flirting with anyone."

"Oh, please." She rolled her eyes at him, then smiled as she set down a glass of whiskey in front of a cowboy sitting at the bar. Lowering her voice, she said, "You can't help yourself. I get it."

"Get what?" After moving aside two filled pitchers, he read Elaine's order ticket and started on the next one. "We're only friends, right? So why should you care?"

"Right." Mallory leaned down to scoop ice from the steel bin, and he got a brief glimpse of her black bra and creamy skin. Knowing he couldn't touch was pure torture. "It's just that—well, I was sort of rethinking things about us, but then I saw you hitting on Heather and—"

"Whoa. Wait a minute. I was not—" He remembered where they were and how easily they could be overheard. He shut off the tap and crouched so he was eye level with her. "I was not flirting with Heather. She was hitting on me because you put her up to it."

"I most certainly did not." She started to straighten but he caught her arm. "She asked if we were together and I said no. That's all."

"So you didn't tell her she could have me all to herself?"

"Yeah, and that." Mallory arched a brow. "But it didn't mean anything."

The mocking tone of her voice got his attention. He'd mentioned something in that vein about them having had sex. Was she still pissed about that?

Something she'd started to say finally registered. "Rethinking things?"

"How long are you here for?"

"A week. What things?"

She slowly met his eyes. "About us," she said and cleared her throat. "About whether or not we should include sex—"

"What are you two doing down there?" Elaine loaded

pitchers onto her tray in between giving them funny looks.

"Trying to have a private conversation, if you don't mind," Gunner said irritably.

"I don't," Elaine said with a laugh. "But you have a roomful of customers who might."

"Oh, God." Mallory pulled her arm away and shot to her feet.

People sitting at the bar either looked confused or were grinning.

Gunner ignored them. "So you're saying we can—"

Mallory gasped. Head down, she muttered, "Stop talking. Right. Now."

He waited until she finished filling orders and then tugged her to the other end of the bar where no one was sitting. "Just to be clear...we're talking about sex, right?"

Her eyes blazed. Reddish-gold flames seemed to leap from the dark green depths. "Not if you keep embarrassing me we're not."

"No one can hear us."

She swept a quick gaze to her right. "I have conditions."

"Okay."

"No one can know. Not Ben...not anyone," she said, and he nodded, pissed that she thought she needed to tell him that. "And you can't be sleeping with other women from around here. If that's not going to work for you—"

"Jesus." Gunner frowned. "I wouldn't do that."

She searched his face, looking for who knew what. Finally she said, "Fine. We have a deal."

Gunner just smiled, and kept his mouth shut. Damned if he'd give her a single reason to change her mind.

7

At 1:00 A.M., dead on her feet, still stewing over whether she'd made the right decision to have sex with Gunner, Mallory handed the front door key to Elaine. "Would you mind?"

"Thought you'd never ask." Looking wiped out herself, she stopped to give the last customer a nudge in the ribs. "Come on, Earl. Get your butt moving. I'm not telling you again."

The older man ignored her at first. But when he saw Elaine put a hand on her hip, he slid off the barstool and grumbled all the way to the door.

Mallory went back to reloading the dishwasher. She'd sent Heather home an hour ago, the second the place had died down. Gunner was straightening tables and chairs and collecting dirty glasses. The man had never worked so hard to get laid in his life, she thought, biting back a smile.

Of course she'd made the right decision. He was going to be in town a whole week. There was no way she'd be able to resist him. That's why she'd left California in the first place. She hadn't counted on him following her. But he had, and there was no point in depriving herself of a week of amazing sex.

Sadly, she figured either way it was going to hurt like hell when he left.

What probably wouldn't happen was them having sex tonight. He looked as though he could go for another six hours. Mallory would be lucky if she didn't keel over halfway home. To think she'd planned on doing more unpacking. Forget that.

She closed the dishwasher and tried not to stare as he approached, looking so fine in old jeans and the blue T-shirt he'd traded for the white one.

"I had that bull covered tighter than a nun's—" Gunner cut himself short and glanced at Elaine coming toward them.

"Go ahead," Elaine said, grinning. "I don't think I've heard this one."

He smiled and deposited a bunch of dirty glasses in the sink. "I even slapped on an out-of-commission sign. But everyone had to have a look."

"That surprises you?" Since the dishwasher was full, Mallory turned on the water and squirted detergent in the sink.

"I've got this," Gunner said quietly and urged her to step aside. "Go put your feet up and count your money."

Elaine sighed and batted her eyelashes at him. "I can forget my husband and kids' names in a second flat. You just say the word, sugar."

"Uh-oh. Do I have to worry about your husband showing up with a shotgun?" Mallory teased, so tired it almost hurt to smile. But she didn't miss Elaine's mischievous little grin. "Why don't you take off? I'll be out of here soon, myself."

Elaine started to argue. But one look at Gunner and she bid them good-night and left.

Mallory hadn't seen his expression, but she could imagine the look that had sent the woman scurrying. "I think I'll take the cash home with me and count it there. I'm so exhausted if I sit down I might not get back up again."

"How far is your place from here?"

"Just a few blocks. I walked."

His dark brows drew together in a frown. He pulled the stop to drain the sudsy water and started rinsing the glasses. "My truck is parked close. I'll drive you."

"It's safe. I'm not the least bit worried."

"You should be," he said, turning to look at her. "I'm guessing the crime rate is next to nothing, but tourism has picked up. And don't forget the area is attracting more Hollywood people."

"Yep, can't trust those Californians," she said and they both smiled.

"I'm just saying…doesn't hurt to be cautious."

She finished emptying the register and stuffed the cash in a worn black leather pouch that had been her father's. A wave of nostalgia swept over her. The Renegade had been her home for more than half her life. She'd hated math in school but learned to add, subtract and multiply by helping with the bank deposits and ordering booze.

"Mallory?"

She looked up and saw that the glasses were dry, and so were his hands. How long had she been staring at the pouch? "I figure I'll come in early tomorrow and sweep," she said, busying herself with organizing the credit card receipts.

"Thinking about the Renegade?"

She shrugged, keeping her eyes lowered. "And my dad, the gang… I wonder how long it took for Moose and Jerry to find a new dive."

"They're probably still sitting in some liquor store parking lot drinking beer and arguing over it."

With a laugh, she looked up. Her heart missed several beats.

The warmth in his eyes…she'd never seen that before. Nothing sexual. It was more like…

God, she really was tired.

He tossed the used towel in the plastic bin with the others. "What else can I do to get us out of here?"

"Nothing, really. I assume you're staying at Ben's? You can take off."

"I'm driving you home."

"Gunner, what I said earlier… I'm not reneging, but I'm bushed and I have boxes all over—"

"I know." He moved closer and put his arms around her. "I'm not expecting anything." He brushed his lips across hers and hugged her to his chest. It felt so good burying her face against his neck. "You need sleep. We both do. Let's get you home and we'll go from there."

Sounded good in theory. But once they were alone? Pressed this close, already her body had perked up. He didn't wear aftershave or cologne, but then he didn't need to. His rugged outdoor scent enticed her to stay where she was even without the feel of his warm solid chest and strong arms.

"And by that I mean, after you're tucked in, either I go on back to Ben's or sleep on your couch. How's that?"

"Oh, you think I'm that fancy?" She laughed. "I wish I had a couch."

"Okay, no problem. We'll share the bed."

She leaned back to look at him.

Gunner smiled. "To sleep. That's it."

"Uh-huh."

"I swear." He shrugged. "Unless you start something."

She just shook her head. "Let's go."

The ride took three minutes, including the short walk to his truck. Had she hoofed it all the way, she might've made it home by dawn. She was that exhausted.

She opened the front door, then glanced back looking for Gunner. He stood near the gate where she'd left the small U-Haul parked, and apparently unlocked, because he was peering inside at her belongings. It would be easy to call out a good-night to him. He might not like it but he wouldn't push the issue.

Instead she patted the inside wall, found the switch and turned on the porch light. The rest of the houses on the street were dark.

Gunner quietly closed the U-Haul and joined her. "Okay if I come in?"

Say no. "Sure." She was hopeless. "But be warned."

She led him inside and then glanced around as if it was her first time seeing the place. Jeez, it really was a mess with boxes stacked everywhere, some opened, their contents lying across the wood floor. Nothing embarrassing. As far as she could tell.

"You have a lot of stuff," he said, his gaze sweeping over the old brown recliner, the floral love seat, a pair of small tables.

"Not really. I did a lousy job packing. I should've used fewer boxes."

"I don't know why you were in such a hurry. There was still time on your lease."

She knew what he was leading up to and she was not about to have that conversation now. "This was so stupid to come here. I still have my room at The Boarding House."

"Is that the low white building on the edge of town?"

Sighing, she nodded, wondering where she'd left her makeup and toothbrush. She'd been too excited about getting the house today and couldn't remember where anything was.

"Is your bed here?"

"Yes." She groaned when she remembered it wasn't made up. "I don't even know where the linens are."

Gunner brushed aside the hair that had escaped her ponytail. His fingers lightly grazed her cheek and then the side of her neck. He rested his hand on her shoulder. "I see some gray sheets by the fireplace. I'll take care of the bed."

"You're going to a lot of trouble for nothing."

"I thought you wanted to sleep," he said, his voice absent any trace of mocking.

She stared into his hot, intense gaze and warned herself not to be foolish. She cleared her throat and looked away, trying to ignore her body's reaction to his touch. To the rasp in his voice. To the evening stubble shadowing his jaw. To those hypnotic gray eyes that seemed to see clear down to her soul.

They were alone. Standing close.

She knew this would happen.

"Look, if it helps," he said, lowering his hand, "even if you begged me I wouldn't have sex with you right now."

Mallory laughed.

"You want to show me to the bedroom?" He gathered the sheets and uncovered a pillow. "Or shall I find it myself?"

Without a word, she headed down the short hall, aware he hadn't searched for a second pillow.

The house was over fifty years old so both bedrooms were small. So was the single bathroom. But it was perfect. The porch and backyard made up for a lot.

"How'd you get a queen bed in here?" Gunner stood at the door, his broad shoulders filling up the doorway. "Couldn't have been easy."

"Grace helped me."

He gave her a sharp look. "Today?"

"This morning." Mallory slid in between the bed and the wall with the window. "Toss me the fitted sheet."

Gunner left the linen on a box in the open closet and then shook out the bottom sheet over the mattress. "What, no neighbors came rushing over to help? Out of nosiness if nothing else."

"Wow, how quickly you've forgotten how small towns operate. They probably knew I was moving in before I did," she said and got a smile out of him. "But yeah, a couple of them caught me on my way to the bar."

"Think you'll get used to it?"

"I'd better," she said, keeping focused on her task. The conversation could easily slide into dangerous territory. "I put everything I have into the Full Moon."

Gunner followed her lead and stayed quiet until they'd tucked in the top sheet and lightweight blanket. "Do you have a lease?"

"For the house? Or bar?"

"Both."

"Why?" She thought about opening the window, then

reconsidered. "You don't think I'll make it here?" she said, watching for his reaction as she came around the bed.

"You seem to be doing okay so far." He shrugged, his mask in place, guarding his thoughts.

"Having Ben here helps. And I really like Grace—"

"Why didn't you call me?" he asked, and she froze, unprepared for the direct question. "This morning…to help you move."

"I didn't call anyone," she said with relief. "Grace was on duty and stopped by while I was bringing in boxes." Mallory grabbed the pillow and kept her gaze lowered as she stuffed it into its case. "Where's the other one?"

"I haven't looked. You sleep with two?"

"No." She hugged the thick fluffy pillow to her chest and forced herself to meet his probing eyes. "I meant for you."

He reached out a hand, and she squeezed the pillow tighter.

"It's a short drive to Ben's," he said, briefly touching her cheek. "I don't want to make you uncomfortable."

"Look, the offer is still sleep only. In five minutes I'll be dead to the world."

"Okay." He nodded. "I'll go find that pillow."

This was going to be so weird, Mallory thought as she closed herself in the bathroom. Her toiletry bag and sleep tee were there, thank God, and she wasted no time getting her teeth brushed and her face washed. She considered a quick shower, but no, that might wake her up. As if knowing Gunner would be lying next to her wasn't enough to keep her wired.

She listened to him moving around in the living room, then heard him in the kitchen. It really was a tiny house but she looked forward to fixing it up and putting her stuff out. After pulling on the Daffy Duck T-shirt, she stared into the mirror. Gunner had never seen her without makeup before. She didn't wear all that much, but the liner and mascara made a big difference.

So what? This wasn't a date. Hell, he might get bored and drive to Ben's, anyway.

Leaving the bathroom door open, she went straight to her bedroom. She already knew he wouldn't be there because she'd heard him in another part of the house. She hoped he wasn't touching her stuff. Mostly because she wasn't sure what he might find.

Nah, Gunner wouldn't snoop.

She turned off the light and slanted the bedroom door to redirect the beam coming from the living room. Sighing, she slipped between the cool, clean sheets. She turned on her side and closed her eyes. The blanket was lightweight but still too much. She kicked it off and flipped onto her stomach.

It was a mistake not to open the window.

Montana evenings were a lot cooler in July than they were in southern California. But she'd had an air conditioner in her old apartment.

Forcing the window open made an awful noise. But it didn't disguise the sound of the front door closing. So he'd decided to go to Ben's after all. Fine. She liked having the whole bed to herself.

Who was she kidding? She was disappointed. Which was stupid. Though he could've said something before he'd taken off.

She stopped midway down the hall. "Oh." She backed up as he advanced, a pillow under his arm. "I thought you left," she said and wished she hadn't when he frowned. "I'm done in the bathroom. Sorry I don't have an extra toothbrush."

"I had one in my truck," he said, glancing down at her sleep shirt with a faint smile. "And not for the reason you think."

"Me?" She eyed the small leather bag in his hand. Probably his one-night-stand kit. "I'm not thinking anything."

He stopped at the bathroom, just as she felt the bedroom door at her back. They silently eyed each other like adversaries in a grudge match.

"I don't think I've seen your bare legs before," Gunner said, making sure he got his fill of them now.

When he looked up, she knew he was thinking about that night. In the back room of the Renegade. When he'd stripped off her jeans and panties and spread her thighs.

They'd left the lights off that night. Moonlight had shined through the glass windows in the front of the bar but only a meager glow had made it to the back. They hadn't seen much of each other. But his hands and mouth had explored every part of her with a thoroughness that made her clench every time her mind relived the experience.

She'd taken her own liberties. Using her hands and tongue until she'd memorized every contour of his chest and the hard glutes that made him look amazing in jeans. And, she was quite sure, without.

"Good night," he said, his voice deeper, huskier. "In case you're asleep when I come to bed."

She just nodded, and tried to swallow.

Looking into his lust-darkened eyes, feeling the raw rasp in his voice grazing her skin, all she could think was *fat chance*.

8

GUNNER MOVED QUIETLY into the bedroom and paused so his eyes could adjust to the darkness. Convinced she'd be asleep by now, he had turned off every light, including the one from the hallway.

She'd kicked off the covers and lay curled on her side, her T-shirt riding up high and exposing tiny pink panties. Her eyes were closed and her breathing was the soft, even rhythm of a deep sleep. It would've surprised him if she'd been awake. Not only had she looked exhausted, but he'd deliberately given her a forty-minute head start. For both their sakes.

The cold shower he'd taken hadn't quite cut it. He'd calmed down a bit, only after giving his body some relief. But it hadn't stopped the arousal from building again. Not when images of Mallory kept filling his mind.

And now, here she was, in the flesh, her honey-colored hair spread across the pillow, her lips slightly parted. A shaft of moonlight shining through the window fell at an angle from her knee to her shoulder.

Just looking at her long bare legs made his skin hot and tight. If it became a problem, he'd sleep on the floor.

Outside the mountain air was pleasantly cool. Between Mallory's window and the two he'd opened in the living room, they were picking up a nice cross breeze. He thought about pulling the covers over her.

Maybe in a minute.

Leaving the bedroom door open, he hung his T-shirt on the doorknob and made the decision to keep his jeans on. It wasn't easy. He'd like to think he wouldn't disturb her much-needed sleep. That he'd keep his word and his hands to himself. But better to play it safe.

He slid in next to her and she woke for a moment, lifting her head and turning to look at him. Her lips curved in a brief smile before her eyes drifted closed again. He stayed perfectly still, waiting, hoping she'd roll over to face him.

Disappointed, he watched her turn back toward the wall. Just as well. Better not to test his willpower. A second later she adjusted her pillow and stretched out on her back, eyes still closed.

She wasn't wearing a bra.

Her round breasts strained against the thin T-shirt. A splash of moonlight revealed what he already knew— the size and rosy color of her nipples. He flashed back on how they'd blossomed under his tongue. The temptation was almost too much.

With a muted curse, he pulled up the covers and tucked them around her as a barrier between them. Yeah, right. As if a few layers would stop him. She stirred when he brushed a tangle of hair away from her face, but she didn't wake up. She looked so young without makeup. Young and vulnerable.

That discovery had stunned him the most the night they'd had sex. Yeah, the fact that he'd made the move on her in the first place was surprising. But it was her initial streak of shyness that evening that had shocked him. Made him realize he hadn't known her as well as he'd thought.

Mallory always came off as tough. She'd practically cut her teeth in the Renegade, exposed to things no child should've seen or heard. The wild bikers and reckless, freewheeling stuntmen had rarely censored themselves in her presence. She should've been going to school dances and football games, learning how to kiss in the backseat of a car.

Not illegally serving drinks because her father had gotten smashed. Or being forced to face rowdy drunks. Usually a few regulars had rallied to her side, but she'd never been one to wait for backup.

Yep, Mallory had put up quite the front for a woman with a streak of vulnerability as wide as the Grand Canyon.

Years ago he'd known another young girl who'd been forced to grow up too quickly. Krista had been all of thirteen when they'd crossed paths, a runaway, living on the streets just like him. He'd been sixteen at the time and had tried to look out for her as best he could, but he'd lowered his guard and things had turned out bad for her.

He'd thought about her over the years, though at first he'd tried to push her out of his mind. The guilt had been too much to bear. Now he understood there was nothing he could've done for her. But still, he should've known better. You couldn't let someone down if you didn't let them get too close in the first place.

Mallory shifted a little, but her eyes stayed closed.

One minute was all he'd give himself to watch her sleep. And then he had to roll over, face the opposite wall. The more he'd thought about it, the clearer the truth had become. She hadn't moved to Blackfoot Falls because of the high California rents or for a business opportunity. She'd been trying to get away from him. He just couldn't understand why.

He replayed the last few minutes of that night at the Renegade. Their goodbye had been rushed. It had been after 3:00 a.m. and his flight to Argentina left at 7:00. With only two and a half hours to pack and get to the airport, he'd known he'd been cutting it close. But after they'd gotten dressed and said goodbye for the third time, they'd kept kissing.

Somehow they'd made it to the door, her clinging to him and Gunner unwilling to do anything but hold her tight. Finally, Mallory had pulled away and shoved him out the door. She'd been laughing and telling him he had to go.

For the first time in his life he'd considered shining on the job. Pretending he was sick and letting the stunt coordinator replace him. It would've been a bad move. He'd been lucky to work on that particular film. Big director, big budget, lots of hazard pay. But had he known the projected three-week job would stretch to four, he would've backed out on the spot.

He wondered what would have happened if he'd come clean the next day when he'd called her from Argentina. If he'd admitted he had feelings for her and that he wanted more than...

Shit.

That was part of the problem. He didn't know what he wanted and she'd probably heard the hesitation in his voice. Or maybe she didn't want to be tied to him.

In the past few months, it had gotten so he'd resented working away from LA. That's when the calls had started with more frequency. About every other day, between shots, anytime he hadn't been needed on the set and he'd known the Renegade wouldn't be too crowded. Always him calling her. Had he pushed her away?

He stared at her parted lips. This was a damn stupid idea. Sleeping in the same bed? With him ready to burst from weeks of pent-up worry and frustration?

Gunner felt like a stick of dynamite, tight and ready, and Mallory was the flame that could set him off.

A CHILLY BREEZE swept over Mallory and she reached for the covers. The sheet and blanket were tangled at her feet and she couldn't seem to jerk them free. Another source of warmth beckoned her. She huddled closer to it and opened her eyes, blinking in the semi-dark, unfamiliar room.

The cool air was coming from the open window. But this wasn't The Boarding House Inn. She started to tense then remembered she was in her new place, in her own bed, next to—

She bolted upright and stared down at Gunner.

He shifted at her sudden movement, but his eyes stayed closed and his breathing remained deep and even. He looked so peaceful lying there on his back, completely at ease with the world. She'd never seen that relaxed expression on his face before. Maybe he always looked like that when he slept, though she doubted it. His life was fueled by adrenaline.

That he'd left on his jeans made her smile. But he was shirtless, and she could just make out the smidgen of dark hair across his chest, tapering down to his flat stomach.

He must've missed the warmth of her body because he moved closer. His skin was cool where it touched her thigh. She thought about getting up to close the window, but she hated to wake him. After working four weeks abroad and then racing to Montana, he must be exhausted, too.

With a shiver, she freed the covers, and then pulled them up as she snuggled down. She rubbed her cheek against his shoulder and a faint smile tugged at his mouth. He didn't wake up, though, not then, and not when he slid an arm underneath her and pulled her closer.

Lying on her side, with his arm curled around her waist, she gently laid her head on his shoulder and placed a palm on his chest, against the warm skin and hard muscle, the sprinkling of soft dark hair, the small mole below his left nipple.

It stunned her to realize she'd memorized so much about him. And that was after being with him only that one night. They'd had sex twice in two hours, and once with most of their clothes on. But it didn't matter. Even blindfolded, she'd be able to identify him by touch, his musky scent, and his...

She snuggled down a little farther, needing to taste him. She licked the upper part of his pec. The salty tang of his warm skin had been imprinted in her mind, as well.

She stared at his flat belly, at the narrow strip of paler skin where the denim rode lower on his hips. While she appreciated the thoughtfulness behind him keeping on his jeans, right now, she wished he hadn't. But then neither of them would be getting any sleep.

Mallory wished she knew what time it was, though

it was still dark so she couldn't have been asleep for all that long. Which meant Gunner had had even less sleep. For what had seemed like forever she'd lain awake, waiting, listening to him move around the house, and then she must've crashed hard.

Slowly she lifted her chin until she could see part of his profile. She really liked the strong jut of his jaw, and he had nicely shaped lips. Wanting to touch him, she moved her hand over his...

"Did I wake you?" he whispered.

Mallory froze. "No, I think it was the other way around," she murmured.

He caught her hand and kissed the back of her fingers as they curled into a fist. "Are you cold?" he asked, his arm tightening around her. "I can close the window."

"I'm fine."

"Try to go back to sleep," he said, the words muffled from his lips being pressed to her hair.

Yeah, like that was gonna happen. He had to be able to feel the fast pounding of her heart. Which meant he was ignoring it. Probably because he wanted to go back to sleep.

And that meant—

"You're thinking too hard, sweetheart."

She looked up just as he opened one eye and smiled. She freed her hand and traced a fingertip around his small, dark nipple. His chest hair was incredibly soft. "How tired are you?"

He opened the second eye. "Fully charged."

Mallory grinned. "You're wearing jeans."

"Yes," he drawled. "What are you getting at?"

"You don't have to do that."

"Yeah, I kinda do."

She followed the arrow of hair to his waistband and skimmed her fingers across his warm skin. Either that was one hell of a hard-on or a trick of the moonlight. "Aren't they sort of—inconvenient?"

"You're going to have to be more specific."

"Do I have to explain the facts of life to you, Ellison?"

His deep, rumbling laughter vibrated through her body, triggering all kinds of tingling within it. "Sure, let's hear it."

Damned if she'd let him call her bluff. "A cannot be inserted into B with your jeans on."

"That's not quite accurate." He sounded wide-awake. "Want a demonstration?"

She dipped her fingers just inside his waistband. "I can take it from here—" She let out a surprised squeak when he moved her hand away and drew her T-shirt up and over her head.

"Just remember who started this," he murmured and rubbed his thumb over her tightened nipple.

Bowing his head, he rolled his tongue over the hard, sensitive tip, then trailed it across to her other breast. After giving it equal attention, he licked a path up her throat and took her mouth with a fierce hunger that made her tremble.

He slowed things down, rubbing his palm up her arm and then sliding his long fingers behind her nape, his tongue stroking hers, teasing, tasting, until she whimpered into his mouth.

With his free hand, he covered her left breast. His touch was light and she pressed her aching nipple into his palm. His mouth lifted into a smile.

Yes, she was impatient. She found his zipper and the

bulge behind it. She shifted because she was going to need both hands for this job.

He broke the kiss. "Wait." He rolled out of bed and quickly shed his jeans and boxers at the same time.

She inched back to give him room, but as he slid back into bed, he hooked an arm around her waist and brought her up against him. His erection felt blistering hot. His whole body was giving off heat and making her dizzy with anticipation.

He buried his fingers deep into her hair, holding her just where he wanted her while he tugged at her lower lip, nibbling gently, teasing her mouth open, then slipping his tongue inside.

His heart hammered hard but at a steady pace, almost as if he was in complete control of each beat.

It pissed her off. She could no more regulate the wild pounding in her chest than she could stop the moisture from gathering between her thighs.

He leisurely swept a hand down the curve of her back. Just before he got to her panties, he made an equally unhurried return trip. The sly move pumped her full of anticipation, and then totally messed up her breathing.

Mallory dragged her mouth away from his and whispered, "Condom."

His hand stilled and his heart might have skipped a beat. "Right." He stole a kiss, and then muttered, "Shit," as he rolled out of bed again.

"I have a box. I'm just not sure where it is."

Gunner turned and gave her the oddest look.

"What?" She wasn't a virgin. He knew that. Why wouldn't she have a supply of condoms? She'd bought the box the day after they'd had sex. She wondered what he would've thought of that.

Without a word he picked up his jeans and withdrew a packet from his wallet. She took in the muscled contour of his firm ass. It was perfect. Damn him, *he* was perfect. That's why sex was such a stupid idea.

He turned back to the bed, and Mallory quickly lifted her gaze. He winked and got out a second packet.

Biting back a smile, she pulled the sheet up to her chin. What she should've done was get rid of her panties, though she was curious as to how he'd do it now that they weren't behaving like two drunk chimps in heat.

No matter how hard she tried she couldn't keep her eyes off his erection. Rock hard, smooth and pulsing, it truly was a thing of beauty.

His cock jerked, and she jumped in response. She forced her gaze up.

One corner of his mouth moved in a slight smile. He stood next to the bed looking down at her, as if he expected her to do something. Maybe he wanted a—

He caught the corner of the sheet and with minimal wrist action most of it ended up on the floor.

She squeezed her thighs together. It was an instinctive response, but that didn't make her feel like any less of an idiot. "I was a little chilly," she said, relaxing against the pillow, watching his gaze move to her breasts.

"I'll close the window."

"That's okay. I'm sure you'll find a way to warm me up."

"I reckon I can," he said, and there was that hint of Texas in his voice. He rarely let it slip, and she'd learned a long time ago not to mention it when he did.

Stretching out next to her, he offered her the packet. She gave him a small nod. "Go ahead."

He dropped it on the mattress. "I'm in no hurry," he

said, cupping her nape with his large hand and claiming her mouth.

His lips were warm and firm, moving lightly over hers. The kiss was nothing like the fevered rush from minutes ago. He took a couple of nips with his teeth, but he wasn't even using his tongue. He just kept adjusting the angle of his head, testing the different ways their mouths fit together.

He traced a finger along the ridge of her collarbone before his hand moved down to cup the swell of her breast. He gently kneaded, his thumb circling her nipple, coaxing it into a tight bud. Lightly plucking at it with his roughened fingertips, he moved his mouth to her other breast. Something about the dual sensations sparked a primal reaction in her, so great, she swore she was going to come from that alone. But he hadn't lingered so she didn't know if it was even possible. She still hoped to find out.

Lifting his head, Gunner slid his hand around to her butt and pulled her more firmly against him. The heat of his erection seared her, sent liquid fire pounding through her veins.

"Warm enough?"

"Almost." She parted her lips and his tongue slid inside and ran along the edge of her teeth, delving deeper and staking its claim.

The tempo was still slow and controlled, but his thumb had returned to her nipple and was moving a little faster now, sending prickles of heat all the way to her core. She wanted him. Wanted him inside her. Wanted him to hold her as tight as he could and fill her until she couldn't take it anymore.

She reached between them and wrapped her hand

firmly around his cock. The taut skin felt silky and smooth and so hot against her palm. She stroked down, then inched back up until she felt the moist crown.

His hand covered hers, stopping her, and then he cut off her protest by pushing her onto her back.

"How is this fair?" she asked, frustrated.

His teeth flashed white. "Nothing in life is fair, Mallory," he said, cupping her jaw. "We both know that."

Their eyes met and he kissed her, slowly, thoroughly, watching her the whole time. Until she'd completely forgotten what she'd been upset about.

He moved on to kiss her breast and slid a slow hand down her body, across her ribs, along the curve of her hip and over her belly, lingering at the juncture of her thighs.

His palm grazed the silky panties, two fingers dipping under the elastic. In a split second, Gunner stripped them down her legs and they were gone.

9

GUNNER STARED DOWN at her pale skin, at the small heart tattoo on her hip. He hadn't noticed it the first time. Racing through stages of semi-naked to buck naked in a mostly dark bar meant they'd probably both missed a lot about each other's bodies.

But he sure as hell knew one thing had changed.

He traced the narrow ribbon of trimmed hair with his thumb. Waxes had different names, and he was pretty sure they called this one a landing strip. "When did you do this?"

"What?" Mallory got up on her elbows and looked down. "Oh." She brought her chin up. "Why do you want to know?"

"Just curious."

"I don't remember."

"Had to be in the past five weeks." He traced his forefinger in the shape of a small triangle, just like the one that had recently covered the area above her clenched thighs.

She dropped back to the pillow. "See, you have a better idea than I do."

Watching her cheeks turn pink fascinated him. He didn't think Mallory ever blushed. Could be a shadow. He stroked her petal-soft face with the back of his fingers. Her skin was warm, but then, so was his.

"And the tattoo," he said, touching the small red image. "When?"

"Years ago. On a dare."

Gunner smiled. That was Mallory. "You choose the heart?" he asked, dragging his fingers down her left thigh.

She gave him a jerky nod, her eyes trained on his roving hand. "I thought it would hurt the least."

"You have any others?"

"No." She shivered when he brushed his fingers across the strip of soft hair. "You?"

He just smiled. What he really wanted to know was when she'd bought the box of condoms. He'd spoken to her right after he'd landed in Argentina. She'd sounded okay, a bit shy, but that hadn't surprised him.

Mallory wasn't as sexually experienced as he would've guessed. No, she hadn't been a virgin, but he had a feeling she hadn't slept with more than two or three guys. Made sense the more he thought about it. The Renegade had been her home since she was a kid. After Coop's death, she'd kept the bar open at all hours just within the law.

That left little opportunity to meet anyone. Not even at the bar. Her customers tended to be older and too wild. And she wasn't the type who went for balls-to-the-wall sex in a public bathroom, or in a private corner of the bar. Yet he'd done that to her. Took her right there in the back room of the Renegade.

And he'd always regret it. Not that they'd had sex. Only that that had been their first time together.

Shifting so he was more on his side, he tested the seam of her thighs with light finger strokes, hoping she'd open for him. "Why did you push my hand away?" she asked, sending quick looks at his cock pressed against the outside of her thigh. "Was I doing something you didn't like?"

Gunner laughed, then felt like shit when she turned her face away in embarrassment. "No. I liked it. Too much." He slipped his finger between the soft flesh of her inner thighs, to the edge of her damp folds, and her attention centered on his hand. "I want to go slow and easy this time. So you don't think I'm some wild, out-of-control caveman."

Mallory looked at him and burst out laughing. "You think slowing down will change my mind?"

"Hey, watch it," he said and used the distraction to gain entrance.

Gasping when his finger met her wet heat, she grabbed his cock. And squeezed him a little too tight. He'd ride it out, though, if he could, without becoming a soprano for life.

He worked in a second finger and her grip tightened. Okay, this wasn't going to work.

"You think that's a joystick?" he said mildly, nodding at her hand.

"What? Oh," she murmured on a husky moan, relaxing her hold and parting her thighs.

"That's right," he whispered, urging her to spread her legs wider while he changed positions. "Open for me, sweetheart."

Mallory accommodated him, but only by inches at a

time. She clutched his pillow even before he pressed a kiss to the slim opening of her folds. She was wet and slick, more than ready for him, and inhaling her seductive scent threatened the last vestige of his control.

But he was determined to be patient, even if it killed him, knowing it damn well might.

He explored gently just with his finger, rubbing, teasing and gliding around the slippery texture between her lips. Her squirming was going to do them both in before he was ready. Lightly he pinched her nipple and she stilled for a moment.

Without withdrawing his finger, he shifted and touched his tongue to her other nipple, and sucked it into his mouth.

WHAT THE HELL? This was going slow?

Mallory pulled the corner of the fitted sheet off the mattress. If Gunner didn't stop, she was going to come. Yes, that's what she wanted.

Just not so soon.

His finger hadn't penetrated her yet, nor had he narrowed his efforts on her clit. But he wouldn't let up, kept sliding his finger around, the occasional brush against her clit bringing her that much closer to orgasm.

Oh, God. What was he doing to her—

He covered her nipple with his mouth. After a few gentle licks, he sucked hard, drew back to look at it, then blew warm breath on the moist flesh before sucking it into his mouth again. "Gunner, wait," she whispered, her voice so wrecked she didn't think he could understand her. "Please, Gunner." Completely mixing up the signal she was trying to send, she arched into his mouth and bucked against his finger.

Something suddenly felt different.

Tensing, she stilled.

A tendril of pleasure wound gently through her body.

A second later the orgasm ripped through her. Making her hot. Feverishly hot. One after another the spasms rolled through her, robbing her of breath. She tried to gulp in air. Every move intensified the storm raging inside her.

He pushed his finger deeper inside, and she grabbed ahold of his hair. His mouth stayed on her breast, his lips tugging lightly at her nipple, laving it with his tongue, and then raining soft wet kisses on her burning skin.

Her body finally started to settle. At least her chest and head didn't feel as if they were about to explode.

Gunner untangled her clutching fingers from his hair and swung his legs off the bed.

Mallory shot upright. "Where are you going?"

"Don't worry," he said, leaning over her and kissing her lips. "I'm not finished with you yet." He lifted the top sheet and found the condom near her knee.

"Oh." She fell back against the pillow. No, she supposed he wasn't done. His erection hadn't gone down, not even a little. If anything he'd gotten harder.

Her hips lifted in response. The thrill of knowing what was in store for her made her skin tingle. Her breasts were sensitive, her right nipple almost unbearably tender. And yet she still yearned for the moist heat of his mouth sucking, nipping. Touching the tip of her other breast, she rubbed her thumb back and forth, feeling the flesh tighten.

Briefly her eyes drifted closed. When she opened them, she saw Gunner watching her. Only then did she become fully aware of what she was doing. She started to lower her hand…but then she saw the *way* he was looking at her. As if she was the most beautiful, most desirable woman on the whole planet.

The moon was trekking across the sky but had left enough light that she could see his lips were damp, his nostrils flared. And maybe his passion-darkened eyes were more her imagination than reality, but there was no question he wanted her. If nothing else, his pulsing erection proved it.

Her breathing hitched. She wanted to touch him. Hell, she'd longed for this moment for weeks. The minute after he'd raced out of the Renegade to the airport, she'd started missing him. It had taken two days to snap out of the dream. To realize she was being a fool and sliding headlong into heartbreak.

But this was different. Gunner would be leaving soon. Probably for good. He'd be out of sight and out of mind in no time. She understood exactly what she was doing. Enjoying him while she could, that's all.

He got back on the bed, one knee first, his erection nearly within reach. She turned onto her side. This time she wouldn't let him push her hand away. Or her mouth.

Too busy gearing up to take him by surprise, she missed the part when he'd torn open the packet. Before she could object, he rolled on the condom.

She watched, fascinated. The rubber was snug, of course, and she wondered how much pleasure the act of putting it on gave him. Shuddering, she also wondered about the size of the condom. Extra-large? "I wasn't ready for you to do that."

"Why not?"

"I had plans."

"Such as?" Amusement tugged at one corner of his mouth.

"Too late now."

He brushed the hair away from her face with a gentle hand. "Then I'll finish what I started," he murmured and put his mouth over hers.

There was nothing gentle about the kiss. His tongue dove deep seeking hers, demanding a response she more than willingly gave. She kissed him back, hard, matching his fervor, showing him she was ready for anything.

Their mouths lost contact. All of a sudden she was on her back, her thighs spread, as Gunner loomed over her. Bracing his elbows on either side of her, he rested his hips against hers, the weight of his body pressing her into the mattress. His hard length pulsed against her belly.

"I missed you," he said, and her heart thumped. His mouth hovered just above hers, his breath warm and soft on her face. "You're calling the shots, sweetheart. Whatever this thing is, we'll do it your way."

Mallory didn't understand what he meant. And when he kissed the side of her neck, lingered on the spot behind her ear, she was pretty sure she didn't care.

She wrapped her arms around him and rubbed her palms up his back, all the way to the powerful muscles across his shoulders. He moved his hips against hers, his erection growing hotter by the second. Cupping her hands around his hard ass, she pulled him against her as forcefully as she could.

His grunt was part frustration, part laughter.

All she cared about was that he got down to business. *Holy shit.*

She gasped on impact.

Gunner hadn't even entered her all the way yet.

Maybe it was because she was squeezing so tight she'd maimed him for life. But his whole body froze.

"Are you okay?" he asked, remaining partway inside her but staying completely still.

"Yes, dammit. That was a good noise, not a bad one." Impatiently she lifted her hips.

He thrust hard, pushing himself in as far as her body would allow him to, this time ignoring her moan. After a moment, he withdrew halfway, and pushed in again.

Mallory clutched his arm and wrapped her legs around his waist. She felt his biceps and shoulder muscles straining as he moved inside her. He'd found his rhythm but she had the feeling he was holding back. Wanting more, she arched against him. Why wasn't he going faster?

"Kiss me," she whispered, surging up to meet him halfway.

Gunner leaned forward. Her nipples grazed his chest as their lips touched. With a sharp inhale, he slid his hands underneath her, gripping the fleshy softness of her butt and lifting her into his thrusts.

He didn't slow or hesitate. Just delivered thrust after hard, glorious thrust until she couldn't breathe. Couldn't do anything but whimper and moan.

His ragged breaths felt cool on her damp skin. Yet inside she was burning up. Every little thing seemed magnified, but she'd already come once. She wasn't sure if it could happen again.

"Are you close, baby?" Gunner's control was slipping. She heard it in his voice, felt the desperation in his grip.

She sucked his tongue into her mouth and he groaned. His control shattered. Tremors overtook his body. As he threw back his head, cords of muscle strained in his neck. He was too strong for her, but she refused to let go, hanging on to the faith he wouldn't hurt her. Despite the savage look on his face. So she clung to him, digging her fingers into his damp skin, holding him as tight as she could, loving the way he trembled in her arms.

Without warning the first shimmer of pleasure burst from someplace deep in her core. The sensation rippled through her body, infusing her with a warm tingle that spread through her limbs. Her heart thudded wildly and she tightened her hold on Gunner. Together they rode out the storm crashing over them.

When things started to calm, he dropped to his elbows, gazing down at her and sliding his fingers through her tangled hair. Cradling her head in his large palms, he lowered his mouth and brushed his lips across hers.

He murmured soft words she couldn't hear. Her name was the only utterance she could make out, whispered so reverently she thought she might be mistaken. They kissed again before he rolled off and fell onto his back beside her.

It was a long time before she could move. They were both wiped. Briefly, she considered forcing herself to get up and close the window. The early-morning air was chillier than before, and their bodies had cooled considerably.

Mallory wasn't at all insulted that he'd fallen asleep so quickly. If anything she was a little jealous. They both desperately needed the rest, and after that workout, she should be down for the count, as well. Normally her problem was an inability to turn her brain off.

Tonight was different. Filled with a sense of contentment, she snuggled against Gunner. The feeling was odd, almost surreal. But it felt so good that she didn't want to ruin things by going to sleep.

Evidently she had no choice.

Mallory realized she'd dozed when she woke with a slight start. Gunner was lying next to her, on his side, with one heavy leg thrown over her. A strong, muscled arm curled possessively around her waist.

He didn't so much as twitch when she picked up his arm and laid it on his side. His leg was trickier but she finally untangled herself, which wasn't an option at this point. She needed to go to the bathroom.

She saw the pinks and grays of dawn streaking the sky as she closed the window and the blinds. Whether or not she went back to sleep, Gunner shouldn't be disturbed. Soon he'd be making the long drive back to Valencia. Well, in a week. And already she was dreading the goodbye.

She should be used to it. Everyone she'd ever cared about had deserted her. First her mother, then her father ten years later. And no, dying was no excuse because he'd brought an early death on himself by boozing and ignoring his doctor's orders.

She swore stuntmen, even ex-stuntmen, were a different species altogether. Always testing the limits of their endurance and always shocked to learn they weren't invincible. Years after his accident, Coop had still refused to accept his reality. No wonder her mother had ditched him. Mallory just didn't understand why her mom had left her.

After visiting the bathroom, she knew trying for more sleep was useless. She was too pissed at herself for sinking into a shitty mood of her own making. So she put on a pot of coffee and surveyed the living room.

Nothing had magically unpacked itself or found a new home on the mantel. But she could see what Gunner had been doing besides looking for his pillow. He'd broken down empty boxes and piled them in the corner near the door. The unopened ones were neatly lined up close to the recliner, stacked two-high so she wouldn't always have to bend.

All the bubble wrap and wadded newspaper she'd left scattered across the floor had been picked up. She felt an urgent need to explain she wasn't a slob. The unexpected delivery of the mechanical bull had sent her rushing to the bar. But Gunner already knew she could be a mess sometimes. She was strict about the bar being clean and uncluttered. Her car...not so much. Something which Gunner liked to point out on occasion.

The braided brown-and-taupe rug wasn't hers. It was something else the owners had left behind. But she'd already inspected it and knew it was clean. He'd found the perfect spot for it.

He'd even moved the love seat to give her more room, and then placed the two small tables in front so it looked as if someone really lived here and hadn't just dumped their stuff and left.

Her coffeemaker was old, and probably needed replacing judging by the snorts and grunts coming from the kitchen. She walked quietly down the short hall, wanting to peek in on Gunner. Of course she'd let him sleep, and maybe later she'd join him. At the mere thought a flicker of arousal stirred low in her belly. Just like that her mood lightened.

He was still in the same position as when she'd left him. Only his arm was curled over her pillow instead of her. She tried not to take it personally. But the truth was, four nights ago his arm had probably been around another woman. The stuntmen who hung out at the Renegade never seemed to lack female attention. Cheating had been on the long list of her dad's faults.

Sighing, she pulled the door closed. Gunner had never been married. He'd made no promises to her or anyone else. That made him a free agent. And who knew if or when she'd ever have such great sex again. As long as she kept herself in check, she honestly didn't think she was asking for trouble. Even if she was jealous of her own damn pillow.

10

GUNNER STOPPED AT the end of the hall the second he saw Mallory. She was sitting cross-legged on the rug in the living room, unpacking a box. Very carefully she unwrapped a framed picture and a few knickknacks. Torn cardboard, strips of tape and pieces of bubble wrap littered the wood floor around her.

The tempting aroma of Colombian coffee called to him, and had probably teased him awake. But she hadn't noticed him yet and it was a rare privilege for him to see her among her personal things, unguarded, her hair down and bouncing off her shoulders every time she moved her head.

He'd always liked her hair. The soft honey color and the fine silky texture of it, and even the two stubborn kinks that she hated so much she kept threatening to whack it all off. It was probably why she wore a ponytail most of the time.

It was 8:20. He wondered how long she'd been up. Must've been a while. He'd picked up all the packing debris last night.

"Hey," he said softly so he wouldn't startle her.

She jumped anyway, before turning toward him. "Was I making too much noise?"

"No." He shook his head. "You should've woken me," he said and walked toward her.

"There's coffee made." She set the picture she'd unwrapped facedown on the table next to some figurines, and started gathering all the paper and bubble wrap she could reach and stuffing it into a box.

"Mallory?" He bent over and squeezed her shoulders. "You seem jumpy."

"I don't mean to." She leaned back to look at him. "What I meant to say is that I'm not. You know, jumpy."

He gazed at her upturned face, at those sweet, rosy lips and dark green eyes. It would've killed him if he'd seen any sign of regret. He crouched and kissed her, keeping it brief so he wouldn't give in to the impulse to lift her in his arms and carry her back to bed. "Good morning."

"We'll see about that…" Her soft laugh soothed him. "Can you believe this mess?"

"Put me to work."

"Maybe. But if you're in a hurry that's okay."

"No hurry at all."

"Why don't you get your coffee first?" she said, with that hint of shyness he'd seen once before. "I left your— The blue mug out for you."

He nodded at hers sitting next to those weird figurines that didn't seem like anything she'd own. "How about I top you off?"

"Thanks," she said and passed it to him. "Just a tad of cream, no—"

"I know, Mallory."

"Oh. Right," she murmured, looking away.

He headed to the kitchen, wondering about the few moments of awkwardness between them. They'd known each other for about as long as he'd known any other living soul, with the exception of his mother, and he hadn't seen her in seventeen years. He knew how Mallory took her coffee, that she loved shrimp but hated any other kind of seafood, drank only *real* colas and none of the diet stuff. And she would sooner have a tooth pulled than face even the tiniest spider. Which said a lot considering how many times she booked and canceled dentist appointments.

The oversize blue mug she'd left by the coffeemaker also said a lot. She'd kept it at the Renegade because she knew he hated puny cups that couldn't hold more than a few gulps. Yep, they knew each other pretty damn well, and it was obvious to him something was bothering her.

Some of the cupboards were open, every one of them bare. Boxes were stacked in the corner, still taped shut. She had a dish towel with big yellow sunflowers on it hanging off the fridge door. Its twin sat folded on the counter. He thought about the floral love seat and daisy-bordered hand towels in the bathroom. *Huh*. She'd never struck him as the flower type.

No other kitchen things were lying around ready to be put away. She still had a lot of unpacking to do. He'd finish unloading the U-Haul, then stick around and help for as long as she'd have him.

Frustrated and confused, he fixed her coffee, adding just the right dab of cream. He left his black and paused to take a sip.

Sex had to be the problem.

Not the physical part. Last night couldn't have gotten any better. He was getting hard just remembering…

And he needed to cut that shit out right now. He couldn't afford to let his brain get fogged up.

He got to the living room and stopped so abruptly that some of Mallory's coffee sloshed over the rim of the mug.

Was that it? Last night he'd sworn to her he wouldn't initiate anything. And he'd stayed true to his word. The way he remembered it, Mallory had started messing around first. But what if he was wrong? What if he'd—?

"Hey, why are you just standing there?" She pushed to her feet and rescued her mug of coffee. She was wearing the same Daffy Duck T-shirt. It was slipping off one shoulder. No bra.

He'd have to watch where his eyes landed.

"Gunner?"

He lifted his gaze. "What was that?"

Her expression troubled, she asked, "What's wrong?"

Good question. "Let's sit down. Okay? Just for a few minutes." He gestured to the love seat.

"I'm going to hate this," she muttered. "Aren't I?"

"No." He cleared a spot for them, and then cleared his throat. "I don't think so."

Cradling her mug in both hands, she lowered herself to the love seat and angled her legs away from him as he sat next to her. But she never looked away from his face. Just bit at her bottom lip, distracting him, adding to his frustration.

After taking a quick sip of coffee, he set his mug on the table. "I start kissing you and I'll get carried away. Don't let me do that."

"Um." She frowned, and then cracked a small smile. "Okay."

Gunner took a breath. He had a good idea of what he

needed from her to fill in the missing pieces. Damned if he could come up with a subtle way to ask.

"Go ahead, Gunner," she said softly. "Whatever it is, you can tell me."

He nodded. "How many men have you been with?"

Mallory blinked. Her jaw slackened. Then her startled eyes narrowed to a glare. "How many women have you screwed?"

"A lot," he said, keeping his expression bland, regretting like hell being so direct.

"A hundred?" She shrugged, her gaze steady and pissed. "Two hundred?"

He honestly didn't know. Yeah, he might be a jerk sometimes but he didn't keep track. And even if he had a number in mind, he wouldn't admit it. "I'm not trying to be an asshole…"

"Well, then, you should think about keeping your mouth shut." She stood abruptly, spilling coffee down the front of her shirt and muttering a curse. "Why would you want to know? It's a little late to play big brother, don't you think?"

Taking the mug from her, he set it down on the table next to his. "Oh, I never wanted that role," he said, catching her arm and urging her to sit back down. "You know that, Mallory." He rubbed the soft skin of her inner wrist. "I know you do."

Drawing in a deep breath, she perched on the edge of the seat cushion. The fight seemed to be leaving her, at least for the moment. Hopefully, she'd understand where he was coming from, despite his clumsy first attempt at making his point.

"Why would you ask me something like that?" She searched his face, her eyes so hurt it sliced right through him. "I mean, did I—did I disappoint you or something?"

"Jesus. No." Gunner pulled her closer. "No. It's nothing like that," he said, stroking her cheek, her hair.

She didn't struggle or push him away. Far worse, she sat with her back rigid and her arms limp at her sides, her gaze averted.

Hell, touching her might be adding fuel to the fire, but he couldn't stop himself.

"That night at the Renegade—" He remembered how skittish she'd been at first, but maybe that wasn't the best thing to point out. "You were upset about the lease expiring. I came on strong. I'm sure the last thing you expected was for me to hit on you. Everybody else had left. We were both a little drunk. Maybe you felt like you couldn't tell me to get lost…"

She looked sharply at him. "Shut up, Gunner. That's so stupid. You know better."

One thing was for sure, he'd rather see her pissed off than vulnerable. Pissed off he could deal with. "Look, this is how I saw it. We had sex," he said, and she rolled her eyes toward the ceiling. "And it was goddamn awesome. For me." He raised his hands, palms out, when she looked at him again. "I'm speaking for myself here." He paused, saw she wasn't in a forgiving mood yet, but hey, she was listening.

"The timing sucked, me leaving for Argentina. When I called after I landed, the connection was bad, but you sounded okay. A few more calls, each time you tell me you can't talk. Then, you stop answering altogether. And don't return my calls. I was worried because you were in a funk about the lease expiring. I called Mac. He was working in Asia and didn't know anything."

She stared down at her clasped hands.

Gunner welcomed the silence. He needed a breather since he hadn't planned for all that to come out. And there was something else…something that shocked the hell out of him.

Under all the anger, under all the frustration, all the worry that something had happened to her, he finally realized he'd been hurt. Because she'd left like that. Had just taken off without so much as sending a text. As if he meant nothing to her.

He shifted his gaze to the window, trying to shake the raw emotion making him edgy. Trying to forget the feeling of utter powerlessness he'd experienced and had stuffed down deep every time he'd made a call or checked for messages. He'd never felt like that before and it sucked.

Aware she was watching him, he shrugged, pretended something outside had caught his interest before he continued.

"Then last night, it was great. I thought you were into it," he said, cutting to the chase. "This morning you're acting weird again. If I call later, are you gonna answer your phone?"

Sighing, Mallory laid her hand on his arm. "Only two," she said quietly. "A guy I knew in high school… it was one time the night I graduated. And then Brandon…" She kept her gaze lowered. "On and off for about a year. It was just fast, easy sex."

"Brandon?" He knew that name, but hoped he was wrong. "Not the kid who used to deliver your booze."

She looked up. "He's not a kid. Brandon's my age."

"The dumb-ass with the hula girl tattoo on his arm?"

"He got it when he was eighteen and drunk."

"Come on." Gunner hated that he was actually jealous. Was it because Brandon was a good-looking guy, or because Gunner could put a face to the name? "What kind of idiot goes through the pain of getting inked for a hula girl?"

Mallory studied him with a slight frown, then looked as if she'd just had one of her irritating *aha* moments and laughed. "I can't believe it."

"What?"

"All those videos I've seen of you doing incredibly dangerous stunts, which almost made me pee my pants twice by the way, and you're too chicken to get a tattoo. Afraid it's gonna hurt?"

She tried to ruffle his hair but he ducked.

"I never said that."

"You didn't have to. I figured it out."

"I just don't like 'em." He thought about the small heart on her hip that he'd traced with his tongue. Obviously there were exceptions. "Guess I'm still a cowboy at heart."

Mallory's mocking grin faded and she gave him the oddest look.

"You won't see too many guys around here sporting ink," he said. "I can promise you that."

She tilted her head to the side, studying him. "You don't mention Texas much."

"No," he agreed. "Why are *you* bringing it up?"

"I never knew you considered yourself a cowboy."

"Oh." He rubbed the back of his neck, remembering the night he'd told her about growing up on a ranch in Texas. Though the run-down house and sagging barn hadn't been much. Folks around here would laugh at the place. "You know I like working with horses. Ben and

I used to hang out with the wranglers on the set. That's why Rusty and Kirk started coming to the Renegade."

"And now Ben is here running his own ranch."

"Yeah," he said. "How about that."

"I hope he doesn't start missing the action," she murmured, looking skeptical.

Gunner picked up his mug and stared into the cold coffee. He'd had a similar thought so why did her cynicism bother him? "Brandon," he muttered, shaking his head.

Mallory groaned and shoved his arm. "God. I'm sorry I said anything. I haven't seen him in ages, but I shouldn't have mentioned his name. Anyway, how was I supposed to meet guys? Tell me that. I spent most of my life at that stupid bar. And sometimes I just plain ole got tired of my vibrator."

Gunner choked out a laugh. "But Brandon?"

"Oh, grow up." She sprang to her feet but he caught her hand. "You can't ever say his name again. Do you understand? I'm not screwing around."

She continued to glare at him, even as he pulled her onto his lap. But she didn't say a word when he slid his hand up her silky thigh. She just watched his face, and then bit back a smile when he discovered she was wearing panties.

No sweat. He bypassed them and slipped his hand higher under her T-shirt.

11

MALLORY GASPED. "YOU'RE NOT supposed to kiss me, re-member?"

"Ah, that's right," Gunner said, palming her bare breast. Her nipple was already tight and swollen, and the sound of her sexy little whimper went straight to his cock. "I haven't kissed you yet."

"I think this falls in the—the same category," she murmured, her lids drooping.

"You want me to stop?"

"Just try it, buddy."

Gunner laughed. Although he was going to have to adjust his jeans. And soon.

The large T-shirt slipping off her shoulder needed only a slight tug down to expose her breast. Her eyes flew open and she watched him circle his tongue around the tight bud, sweeping close but never touching it.

He felt her shiver, heard her breath catch. She arched, trying to get him to take her nipple into his mouth. But he continued to tease her, laving the skin around it, pressing soft kisses between her breasts…

Until she started to squirm.

His jeans were too snug for that. Shifting her a few inches to the left did nothing to ease the pressure.

"Hey," he said, lifting his head. "Stop it."

She stared at him with unfocused eyes. "Stop what?"

Gunner smiled at the frustration creeping into her face. The memory of her wounded look earlier tried to intrude. He shook it off. How could she possibly have thought she'd disappointed him?

He brushed a kiss across her lips. "You have to stop moving so much."

The fog was clearing. Her gaze sharpened, and with a slow, devious smile, she moved her hips. "Make me."

His laughter ended in a groan. He caught her waist and lifted her off his protesting cock.

"Oh. Sorry," she said, her eyes sincere. Her voice not so much. "But if you'd been doing your job this wouldn't have happened." She slid off his lap before he could stop her, and sat next to him.

"My job?"

"You were teasing me instead of getting down to business." She pulled up the neckline of her shirt.

Gunner watched her breast disappear behind the fabric and sighed.

"You're right," he said, rallying. "That was wrong of me. My technique needs work." He almost nabbed the corner of her shirt hem before she scooted back. "Come on now…don't be like that. I'll only improve with practice."

Laughing, she captured his hand, held it down with both of hers. As if he couldn't get away if he wanted. "First, let's make sure I didn't injure you," she said, nodding at his straining fly, a tiny twitch at her mouth. "I should check."

It was his turn to laugh. "Then I suggest we find your box of condoms because I don't have any more."

"I just want a quick peek."

"Yeah." He freed his hand, and inched toward her thigh. "Because that won't lead to anything."

Mallory let out a laugh and he made his move, grabbing her arm and tugging up her shirt. But with all her jerking around he couldn't get it over her head.

"We have to find the condoms..." Still laughing, she barely got out the words.

She kept struggling, flailing her arms and muttering threats every time he copped a feel. He took a nice nip of her butt and she swung around, on the offensive.

Something shattered. Something close by.

She went completely still, except for her widening eyes.

Turning to the table, her shoulders sagged. "Oh, no. Not that one."

Two of the little figurines had fallen. Pieces of colorful porcelain lay scattered across the table.

She picked up tiny gold chips and larger purple chunks and set them on her open palm. It broke his heart to watch her trying to match the pieces. Putting those figures back together would take a miracle.

He couldn't see why anyone would want to try. Eyeing the row of survivors, he found it odd she'd collected any of them. They were all kinda ugly, but that didn't matter. Clearly they meant something to her.

"I'm sorry." Gunner picked up a gold shard from the floor. "I'll replace them."

She gave him a grateful smile. "First off, it wasn't your fault. Mine, completely. And anyway—" She stared at the remains on her palm. "They can't really be replaced. It doesn't matter." Her shrug was unconvincing. "I shouldn't have bothered packing them. They're not even worth anything."

Gunner put his arms around her. "They make you happy," he whispered. "They're worth everything."

She briefly glanced up at him, then let him pull her close. "Just so you know," she murmured, burying her face in his chest, "you're still on shaky ground. Don't think you can get away with making me cry."

"Oh, shit. Tell me you're not gonna start bawling."

He got the small laugh from her that he'd wanted, and kissed her hair.

It was a shame about the knickknacks. He hated that it made her sad. But being here for her, holding her in his arms, comforting her, it felt so damn right.

Whatever he'd done to chase her off, they'd get past it. He knew they could. For weeks she'd been afraid of keeping her business together, losing sleep over it, wondering if she would ever land on her feet. And the way he'd raced off to make his flight, she had probably felt abandoned, too. It wouldn't have mattered that she'd known he'd had to go because it was his job and that he was coming back. That he always came back. Emotions were seldom rational.

He needed to remember that himself.

She pulled back, sniffing, and gave him a sheepish smile. "I'm fine. The world hasn't come to an end," she said. But she could barely glance at the ugly little whatnots.

What if she was wrong? What if he could find a way to replace them? To surprise her. It always amazed him how much stuff was available online.

Mallory left his arms but he didn't stop her. He figured she wanted to dab at her eyes and nose.

Giving her a moment of privacy, he crouched for a better look at the row of escapees. "Where exactly did you get these little—" He was almost afraid to touch them. Shit, what if he broke another one? "I'm sorry, Mal, I don't know what these things are. They look like toy soldiers."

She crouched next to him and picked up the blue-and-silver figure he'd been squinting at.

"Dale brought this one back from Taiwan," she said. "And then he gave me this little red-and-white guy two years later."

"Dale? You don't mean Dale Thomas."

Nodding, she picked up two more. "These are from Ray, though I think he found them in Japan."

Gunner knew the two guys, both stuntmen. Last year Ray had retired and hung out at the Renegade every day bitching about having been forced into it. No one had paid any attention to him. Goddamn, he'd worked well into his forties. How many stuntmen were lucky enough to say that?

Ray had also been Coop's friend, so Gunner could see him bringing small gifts for Mallory when she was a kid. But Dale wasn't much older than Gunner. His gifts had to be recent.

Mallory dug into another box. "Oh, and look at this gourd. Someone actually hand-carved these figures. It's from Peru," she said, setting it down and admiring the gourd. "Wayne brought it back last fall."

Gunner nodded. "Impressive," he said, familiar with that particular type of workmanship. He'd seen a variety of clever things tribesmen and artisans in South

America did with gourds. He'd even considered buying a few. It just hadn't occurred to him to bring one home for Mallory.

Watching her unwrap more keepsakes, listening to her explain the countries of origin or what the items meant and who'd given them to her, he felt more and more like shit. It seemed as though every damn stuntman who'd ever worked on location had brought home a memento for Mallory.

Every guy except him.

Hell, of course it hadn't occurred to him. She wasn't the type to want silly trinkets.

Or was he fooling himself? Because the happiness on her face said otherwise.

Maybe she'd accepted the gifts to be polite, then thrown them in storage and had forgotten all about them until she'd moved. "I'm surprised you didn't set these things out at the Renegade."

"Oh, please, I would've been too nervous. You know how some of those guys behave when they're drunk." She swept a happy gaze over her little treasures. "I kept them at my apartment in a display case I had made. It's still in the U-Haul. I didn't want to take a chance on moving it by myself and damaging it."

Gunner wished he'd been more thoughtful. What a piss-poor excuse of a friend he was. He managed a smile. "I'll take good care of it for you."

"I know you will." She rose from her crouched position and kissed the corner of his mouth. "You haven't told me how you like the house."

"It's great," he said, glancing down at her bare feet. "It's perfect for you."

"I know just where I'm going to put the Christmas tree."

He looked up to see if she was joking. "You hate Christmas."

"I don't *hate* it. Not really. The day just always seems so—I don't know—anticlimactic or something."

Hell, everything seemed to be getting weirder and weirder. Including those bright pink toenails of hers. And what were those other things…

"What are you frowning at?" She curled her toes, preventing him from getting a better look. "My nail polish?"

"I'm not used to you being so short. You always wear boots with a little bit of a heel."

"Short?" she said, smiling. "I'm five-nine. I don't think that's considered short for a woman."

He kept staring down at her feet. Dead center on each big toe was a goddamn daisy.

"What are you doing? You're making me feel self-conscious." She moved away from him. "Knock it off or I won't buy you breakfast."

Since when did she have a thing for flowers? Or tacky miniature figurines? And Christmas—what the hell was all that about putting up a tree?

"Well, are you hungry or not?" she asked, giving him a grumpy look.

She'd never been domestic or liked girlie things. Not even as a teenager. But it wouldn't matter to him if Mallory was an aspiring Martha Stewart. No, that was a lie. Too extreme for his tastes. They'd shared jokes about being *scandalously* nontraditional. She'd taken pride in being unable to cook worth a damn.

He met her expectant gaze. Right. She'd said something about breakfast. "You don't have any food here," he said.

"Depends on what you consider an apple and a bag of Oreos." Mallory sighed. "That's why I suggested the diner. Marge's is just around the corner."

"I need more coffee." His empty stomach had growled a protest a minute ago. But now, the thought of food didn't sit well. On his way to the kitchen, he realized he'd forgotten his mug and turned back.

Mallory was standing in the same spot where he'd left her, arms folded, staring at him with a troubled expression.

He thought again about how young she looked without any makeup. "I forgot this," he said, grabbing the mug and holding it up, because yeah, he really needed to point out the obvious. "You want some?"

"Earlier you accused me of acting weird. But now you're doing it."

"Am I?" Gunner set the mug back down, then walked over and put his arms around her. She stiffened and kept her crossed arms a barrier between them. "I admit I'm preoccupied. It's getting late and I'm anxious to get your stuff unloaded, especially the display case."

"I hope you aren't blaming yourself for the accident."

"Nope." He leaned back to look at her. "That's exactly what it was, an accident. When do you have to return the U-Haul?"

"It's paid up for the week."

"What time do you open tonight?"

"At six," she said, and uncrossed her arms when he brushed a kiss across her mouth.

"Then we'd better get moving."

Nodding, she lowered her lashes. But not before he saw the disappointment in her eyes.

Okay, so she knew something was wrong, but how was he supposed to explain? He was confused and pissed off. At himself, not her. She was twenty-seven years old. Could be the age when women began itching to play house, decorate Christmas trees.

Have babies.

The thought scared the shit out of him. Gunner had never even considered having kids. Why would he? He didn't know the first thing about raising them. He'd barely seen his own transient father, so no help there. Same went for Mallory. She'd never had any shining examples, either.

He squeezed her shoulders before releasing her and grabbing his mug. "Coffee first," he said, avoiding her face as he headed for the kitchen. "Then I'll start unloading."

It wasn't in his nature to overreact, especially to an imaginary situation. She'd never said a word about wanting kids. And hell, she could start hanging Christmas lights now for all he cared.

Mallory wasn't the problem.

Jesus. It really bothered him that he hadn't once thought to bring her a simple trinket.

He dumped the cold coffee and poured some fresh from the pot. From the kitchen window he could see clear blue sky stretching all the way to the Rockies. It was a residential street but that didn't stop a boy from riding a palomino right down the middle of it.

Yep, this was cowboy country. Full of respectable, solid, salt-of-the-earth men who would love to give a sexy, beautiful woman like Mallory everything she wanted.

Gunner thought about how he'd raced the whole way to Blackfoot Falls, hoping he could convince her to come back to Valencia. He had a lot of money saved. They could've found her another bar.

Now, he wasn't so sure. He had a feeling Mallory would be better off staying here. She deserved a normal, stable life. And that was the one thing he couldn't give her.

12

"Oh, no. This can't be happening. No. No. No." Mallory clutched the steering wheel, rocking forward, as if the momentum of her body weight could keep her sputtering car going. "Don't do this," she pleaded, petting the dashboard. "Please. I promise to get you washed once a week. And no more candy wrappers on the floor. I swear."

Finally, she gave in and eased her poor old compact off the highway before she stalled out and ended up blocking traffic—although she had yet to see a single car and she was already halfway to Kalispell. So, great.

Terrific.

Wasn't this turning out to be the perfect day? It'd started with a broken water main. No one seemed to know how soon it would be repaired. And no water meant she couldn't open the Full Moon.

Oh, yeah, this was awesome.

The car stopped. Just died, right there, without so much as huffing one last sputtering breath.

She rubbed her face and eyes, and then screamed as loud as she could before glaring through the windshield at the hood. No steam was coming out. Whatever that meant in the grand scheme of things, she chose to take it as a good sign.

This was Gunner's fault. She hadn't seen him for twenty-four hours. Not since he'd helped her unload the U-Haul yesterday. He hadn't come by the bar last night, which surprised her. But that was beside the point. Somehow, he was to blame for her normally dependable Hyundai conking out. She just knew it.

Oh, he'd texted some bullshit excuse that he had business to tend to, and that he'd see her soon. She wasn't stupid. What business could he possibly have in Blackfoot Falls? Not for the first time, she wondered if he'd left town, and she felt her throat constrict. He would've told her if he had to drive back. After their talk and everything, he wouldn't just disappear without a goodbye.

Unless this was payback.

No, that wasn't his style. Gunner didn't pull punches and he had a certain look that could make a strong man quake in his boots. She'd witnessed that steely-eyed expression a few times when he'd put himself between her and a drunk at the Renegade. But something clearly had been bothering him yesterday. His mood had gone downhill in the morning and he'd never quite shaken it off. Not that he'd been short-tempered or grouchy. Just quiet. She'd asked what was wrong. All he'd say was *nothing* while giving her a smile.

She truly hoped he didn't think she blamed him for trashing the little collectibles because she didn't, not even for a second.

Her car breaking down? Yes. This was totally his fault. Somehow.

Grabbing her phone, she climbed out, muttering

curses, and then glared at the back tire, which wasn't the problem at all.

"Why couldn't it have been you? I know how to change a tire." She gave it a kick anyway. Just in case. It was strange how cars and computers sometimes responded to threats.

Though not this time.

Shading her eyes and squinting into the late-afternoon sun, she couldn't see a vehicle coming either way. She didn't want to have to call Sadie. The woman had been so nice and helpful, and she probably wouldn't mind, but she'd already done so much. All Mallory wanted was the phone number for a repair shop. She'd try calling Elaine first.

While waiting for Elaine to answer, Mallory tried to recall if she'd seen a sign in town. There were gas stations on both ends of Main Street. The newer one with the drive-through car wash closer to the Food Mart was fairly large…

She was sent to voice mail, of course. She didn't bother leaving a message and tried Sadie.

Voice mail. Again.

God, she despised the thought of calling Ben. He'd probably come out himself when all she really wanted was a phone number. Or worse, he'd send Gunner to come rescue her.

Or maybe she should just get it over with and call Gunner herself. They were supposed to be friends, after all.

If he was still in town.

He'd said a week, but nothing was keeping him here… right?

If he had left, she didn't want to know. Not now. She

wasn't prepared to hear something like that. It pissed her off that she'd missed him last night at the bar. Thankfully, nobody had noticed her constantly checking her phone or watching the door like a silly little fan girl waiting for Benedict Cumberbatch to arrive. Elaine would've said something.

It wasn't until Mallory had crawled into her bed with an ache in her heart that the realization dawned on her. How foolish she'd been to give up a chance at having her own little haven where she wouldn't be ambushed by memories of him. What an idiot. She'd put out the welcome mat and he'd come right in and marked his territory. Now she wondered how long it would take for her to stop picturing him lying in her bed.

Mallory briefly shut her eyes. She had to cut off the images the second they inserted themselves. The scenery was beautiful and a good distraction. Lots of pine trees and aspens grew along the highway and covered the foothills. And the sky, so blue and clear, not a trace of gray smog.

Filling her lungs with clean mountain air, she began to relax. Think clearly.

Grace was on duty. And as much as Mallory didn't like being a nuisance, she decided Grace was the safest bet.

TWENTY-FIVE MINUTES later Mallory heard the faint roar of an engine and glanced up from playing solitaire on her phone. Coming from the direction of Blackfoot Falls and approaching fast, the dark-colored truck was only the third vehicle she'd seen since Grace assured her someone would be out to give her a tow.

Straightening from a slouched position against her

traitorous car, she shaded her eyes. The late-model truck was charcoal gray. She couldn't tell if it was rigged with a tow, or see if it had California plates. But she'd bet it was Gunner.

Her heart thumped wildly and her pulse quickened. Lately, her body reacted that way every time she saw him. She wondered if that would ever go away.

He pulled up behind her Hyundai, got out and headed straight for her, his mouth tight, his eyes blazing. "You don't call *me*," he said. "You call Grace?"

"Hello, Gunner," she said calmly. "Nice to know you're still in town."

"Did I tell you I was leaving?" He stopped a foot away from her, and boy, was he breathing fire. "Ah, I can see why you might be confused," he said with a ruthless smile. "But I'm not the one who disappears without a word."

"Okay, you can knock that shit off right now." She would've backed up if her butt wasn't plastered against her car. "I didn't ask you to come."

"I believe that was my point," he ground out. Even his dark tan couldn't hide the angry flush in his face. He was about as furious as she'd ever seen him, which didn't make any sense—the trace of fear in his eyes even less so.

She jerked when he wrapped a hand around her upper arm. His grip was a bit tight but she wasn't afraid, just confused. "Remember being worried about acting like a caveman?" She gave his hand a meaningful glance and then met his gaze with a glare.

His slow, arrogant smile stole some of her thunder. "You know what they say, in for a penny—" He caught her other arm and lowered his mouth as he pulled her closer.

A split second before he was about to kiss her, she slid two fingers between their lips, shocking both of them. She drew her head back, while keeping her fingers pressed to his mouth.

He let go of her left arm, his intense gaze boring into her.

"What is wrong with you? Why are you angry with me?" She removed her fingers from his warm lips. "I didn't do anything."

He passed a hand down his face, rubbed his beard-roughened jaw and sighed. "I'm not angry with you."

"Well, what the hell, Gunner?"

A long moment of silence passed before he released her other arm. He stared off toward the foothills, as if he was in another world. The old jeans he was wearing sported several tears above the knee, none she'd mistake for a fashion statement. His faded black T-shirt clung to his damp chest and shoulders, the fit snug from so many washings, and fraying at the hem and seams.

Clearly he'd been doing physical labor. Probably helping Ben at the Silver Spur. Why hadn't he mentioned it?

She sighed, and he looked at her.

"I'm sorry," he said, ducking his head and meeting her gaze. "I really am."

Mallory's breath caught at the sky's reflection in his gray eyes. She'd never seen them turn that sexy color of blue before. "I accept your apology," she said, unable to look away. "Now you can kiss me. If you want."

Gunner didn't answer. It seemed he was trying to control a smile. And then he laughed. "Thank you. I believe I will." He put a hand on her waist, dipped his head and gave her the briefest, most unsatisfying kiss ever.

Confused, she watched him move back.

"I should've washed up before I came. After I look under the hood I'll change my shirt. Not sure how much that's going to help..." he said with a sheepish shrug and another step back.

She thought about admitting she found his musky scent arousing, but decided to leave well enough alone.

"Do you have an idea of what's wrong with it?" He walked around to the front of the Hyundai.

"No, it's been driving fine until today. First, I lost some acceleration. Then it started jerking so I pulled over and it just died."

"Did you try starting the engine again?"

She nodded. "Nothing happened."

Frowning, he left the hood down and walked to the driver's side. "Key's in the ignition?"

"Yep, for all the good that does." She opened the door for him. "You'll need to put the seat back. Or I can try starting it again."

"Afraid I'll stink up your car?" he asked with a wry smile, his eyes on her as he adjusted the seat.

"I like the way you smell." She hung over the door to watch him, and also get a little whiff. "It's kinda hot."

He lifted one eyebrow. "I'm all sweaty."

"I know."

Eyes narrowing, he brushed a kiss across her mouth. His curious, calculating gaze stayed on her face as he slid into the bucket seat. Turning the key didn't do a thing, same as before.

But this time Mallory remained nice and calm. Having Gunner here made her feel a hundred times better.

That he seemed to be having trouble figuring her out was a big bonus.

Finally, he turned away from her and pulled out the key. "Where were you headed?"

"Kalispell."

"To do what?"

"Nothing terribly important." She stood back as he got out, and then watched him lift the hood. "There's a band Sadie thinks I might like so I was going to check them out and see if I can afford them."

Gunner didn't say anything and she couldn't see his face. And then he slammed the hood down. Maybe *slammed* was too strong a word, though he'd closed it with enough force to make her jump.

His blank expression told her absolutely nothing.

"I would've asked you to come with me but I knew you were busy." She paused, just in case he wanted to fill her in on what he'd been up to since yesterday. She cleared her throat. "Do you know what's wrong? With my car."

"Yep." He checked his watch. "Don't you have to get back to open the bar?"

"A water main broke at the north end of town where they're building that new motel. So until it's fixed…"

"Is the construction crew responsible? Or is it a lot of finger-pointing?"

She shrugged. "All I was told is that *maybe* I can open later tonight. I'm not sure it'll be worth it." She looked at her car and sighed. "Unless this sucker ends up costing me a bundle."

"It won't." He squeezed her shoulder then rubbed his palm down her arm. "Tell you what, I'll drive you to Kalispell, buy you some dinner and then we can go listen to the band."

"What about my car?"

"I can fix it, but I have to pick up a part first. Might as well get it in Kalispell." He touched her hair, his voice dipping low and sexy. "Be a shame to waste a free night."

"It would." She was trapped between Gunner and her car. He braced one arm against the door while he played with her hair. The tingling sensation kicked in right between her thighs. "Is this a date?"

Gunner's hand stilled and his eyebrows rose slightly. No doubt she'd surprised him, though nowhere near as much as she'd shocked herself.

"Do you want it to be?" he asked, his voice deep and hypnotic as he tunneled his fingers into her hair and caressed her scalp.

"I think so."

"Then, yes." His hand moved to cup her jaw, lifting it as he lowered his mouth. She was beyond ready for his kiss, when he bypassed her lips and licked the speeding pulse at her neck. His mouth curved into a smile against her skin and he whispered, "This is our first date."

Her pent-up breath came out in a soft whoosh. "You're a bastard."

"I know."

"I changed my mind," she said, lifting her chin. "I'm not going anywhere with you smelling like—"

"The inside of your car?"

"Shut up." She laughed in spite of herself.

His eyes lit with humor, only briefly, and then returned to pure want. "That's why we're checking into the hotel first."

"What hotel?"

"Did I leave that part out?"

"But you couldn't have known—"

"We can book a reservation on the way. Maybe splurge on a suite with a jetted tub?" His lips were back on her neck, trailing kisses and taking gentle nips with his teeth. "How does that sound?"

"Expensive." She let her head fall back, giving him better access. "You forget that I'm a poor bar owner."

His mouth stopped moving but she could still feel his warm breath on her throat. "This is a date," he said. "I'm paying."

"I don't think it works that way anymore."

"It does with me." He reared back to look at her.

Mallory grinned at his adorably insulted expression. Who would've thought Gunner Ellison was old-fashioned? "A hotel would be nice." She caught his face between her hands and stretched up to meet his mouth.

A car horn blasted.

They jumped apart, Mallory banging her elbow against the car door. Speeding past them was a truck loaded with teenage boys jeering and whistling out the windows.

Gunner grudgingly acknowledged them with a half-hearted wave and muttered, "Stupid pricks."

Mallory laughed. "Oh, and you never did anything like that when you were a teenager."

"Hell, I was too busy looking for a place to sleep without getting hassled by the cops."

She just nodded, knowing he regretted the comment, even before he avoided her eyes and dug into his pocket. "Here." He passed her a credit card. "How about you call around while I drive? Don't worry about the cost."

She glanced at the Hyundai parked about a foot off

the highway. "You think my car will be all right here overnight?"

"Your car will be just fine."

"And me, Gunner? Will I be fine, too?" she asked, and wished with all her heart she hadn't. In her mind it had been a joke. But when she saw the flash of pain in his eyes, she knew it wasn't funny at all.

"I'll make sure of it," he said.

God help her, she wanted to believe him.

13

GUNNER HAD ENDED up buying a Western-style chambray shirt that Mallory had chosen for him at a store near the hotel she'd booked for them online. Man, he hated to shop, and when he saw the size of the store, offering everything from cowboy boots to horse feed, he'd been tempted to turn right back around. But with Mallory's help the different departments hadn't been difficult to navigate, and he'd even picked up a new pair of jeans.

The hotel, though, that was a disappointment.

It was nice, relatively new, had a large pool and offered room service. Mallory seemed to like the green-and-mauve lobby decor. It just wasn't what he'd had in mind. To be fair, the hotel boasted two suites on the top floor. Maybe if she hadn't been so stubborn and had booked one of them like he'd asked, he'd have been happier with their accommodations.

If he'd been alone, a firm bed and a bathroom with hot water would do it for him. But he was with Mallory and he'd wanted her to have something fancier. He doubted she'd ever been in a suite in her life.

After his shower, Gunner found her lying stomach-down on the bed, studying the room service menu. The black *skinny* jeans, as she called them, did a first-rate job of hugging her slim thighs and paying homage to that sweet, curvy backside of hers. He was a little sorry he hadn't asked her to join him in the shower. But if she had, it would've ruined his plan. "Did you order anything yet?"

"I don't think we should eat in." She glanced up, widened her eyes and let out a whistle. "Well, look at you. I told you that blue went with your eyes. Come on, turn around, let's see the back," she said, sitting up and motioning with a twirl of her finger, and then giving him the stink eye when he shook his head. "Come on, Gunner. I'd do it for you."

"Like hell."

"I would," she said, but her laugh told a different story. "Please."

Finally, feeling like a damn jackass, he made a quick turn.

"Ooh. Nice ass."

He lunged for her, but she scrambled to the other side of the bed, just out of reach.

"This is exactly why we can't order room service," she said, hugging the large leather-bound menu to her chest as if it would protect her from him.

"You lost me."

"I really want to hear Boot Stompin'. And I don't know when I'll have another opportunity like this."

"Did I say we wouldn't? They don't even start playing for another hour and a half," he said, checking his watch. Either they had to order something, anything, or he'd have to convince her to take a bath. A shower wouldn't give him enough time to duck out.

She was staring at him as if he were a simpleton. "If we order room service, you know as well as I do we'll never leave this room."

Gunner smiled. "We don't have to get naked," he said, though she had a point. One that might've occurred to him, if he wasn't so determined to go buy her that red dress he knew she wanted. "I promise to keep my clothes on if you do."

"So you really think that would work, huh?"

"Only because I know we have all night."

In seconds her eyes darkened to that deep mossy green that turned him on all by itself. Then the tip of her tongue slid across her lips, and damned if she wasn't out to test the give of his new jeans.

Time slowed as they just stared at each other.

Mallory broke eye contact first. And then she sighed, with that sad, lost expression he'd seen before but didn't understand. Was she having second thoughts about their—arrangement? About him?

"Listen," he said, holding up his hands as he moved around the bed to take the menu from her. "I haven't eaten all day. I need to order something just to hold me over until dinner."

"We'll eat now." She glanced around the rust-colored carpet, found her black flats and slipped them on her feet. "Let's go."

Gunner blocked her attempt to pass him. He settled his hands on her shoulders and waited for her to meet his eyes. "Look, we don't have to do anything. And I do mean *anything*. You know that, right?"

She gave him an off look. "That's the second time you've said something like that to me. Do you feel—" Her shoulder lifted in a small shrug. "Obligated?"

"Obligated?" He could see she wasn't joking. But what the hell? Bewildered, he grabbed her hand and brought it to the front of his jeans, pressing her palm against his lingering erection. "Does that feel like *obligation* to you?"

A big grin lit her face. Just like that. As if she hadn't almost given him heart failure. "Well, good." She kept her palm molded to his cock even after he'd removed his hand. "We're on the same page."

He grunted at the subtle increase in pressure on his groin. "Mallory Brandt, if I wasn't so crazy about you I'd strangle you. Jesus." Forced to either step back or start tearing off her clothes, he caught her troublemaking hand and brought it to his lips for a quick kiss. "You mind ordering me a cheeseburger?" he asked, backing toward the door and making sure he had his wallet in his back pocket.

"What about dinner?"

"Right." He was pretty damn hungry but said, "Yeah, better tell them to hold the fries."

Mallory laughed. "No. I meant aren't we going soon?" Her smile disappeared when he put his hand on the doorknob.

"We are. I forgot something while we were shopping. I won't be long."

"What? Now?"

"Yep. It can't wait."

"Let's just stop on our way back."

"I can't take the chance the stores will be closed. So if you wait and sign for room service, it'll save time."

She frowned, clearly not liking the plan. "Why don't I go to the store so you can eat when your food gets here?"

"We need condoms," he said, and watched her mouth form a silent *oh*.

"I'm particular about the brand."

He left her frowning and ran to catch the elevator a kid had just vacated.

Earlier, after he'd paid for the toothbrushes and clothes they'd picked up, he'd found Mallory holding a red sundress up to herself and smiling at her reflection. When he'd tried to buy it for her, she'd shut him down.

She hadn't left an inch of room for argument, forcing him to be sneaky about it. And yeah, she might be pissed at first, but he was going to buy her that red dress.

Dammit.

From the outside Wild Bill's Honky Tonk looked like any other roadside bar. But beyond the heavy wooden door the place was enormous. Booths with red vinyl seats lined two of the walls. Tables and chairs made from solid oak crowded the plank floor and should've made it difficult for the waitresses but, wearing short denim cutoffs and cropped green tops with tennis shoes, the women zipped in and out like real pros, serving both drinks and food from the limited menu.

A basket of roasted peanuts was set on each table once the customers were seated. Mallory had toyed with the idea of doing something like that at the Full Moon. Up until she saw shells clinging to the waitresses' hair and clothes and scattered across the floor.

What she really coveted was the old dark-wood bar itself. It stretched along the entire mirrored back wall, lined with shelves stocked with bottles of over sixty kinds of booze, much of it premium stuff. There were three tap stations, one located at each end and another in the middle. Yet none of the four busy bartenders seemed to be getting in each other's way.

One thing about the place puzzled her. Why the massive dance floor? She liked the band a lot, and everyone else seemed to be enjoying Boot Stompin', as well, but she hadn't seen more than a few couples out there so far.

"Maybe I'm wrong to have dancing," she said turning to Gunner, his arm loosely resting on the seat behind her shoulders in the roomy booth. "Giving up all that revenue-producing space doesn't make sense."

He just smiled at her, not even pretending that he hadn't been watching her. Just as he had all through dinner, their very amazing dinner, complete with wine and candles—the real kind, tall and tapered, not like the votive sitting next to their basket of peanuts.

She was starting to get a complex. "What?"

"Nothing." His fingers brushed her bare arm, just as they must've done a hundred times since dinner.

Predictably, she broke out in goose bumps.

It seemed he was always touching her in some way. Whether he was pressing his leg against hers, or playing with her hair, or planting a brief kiss on the side of her neck.

This new intimacy was sweet and sexy and crazy and scary all at the same time. If she wasn't careful and lost perspective, she'd end up in a world of pain once he left.

"You wait," he said, nodding toward the stage where the band was preparing for their next set. "People are still eating. Another thirty minutes and that dance floor will be packed."

"Maybe, but I still think—" She felt his finger slip underneath the strap of her new sundress, the one that she had expressly told him she didn't want. That had been a lie, but not the issue that had set them on a course of barely speaking to each other for a good half hour. "So, are you purposely trying to remind me that I'm mad at you?"

Gunner's lazy smile made her feel a lot of things, and none of them came close to anger. "Hey, you can gripe at me all you want," he said, trailing his finger along the side of her breast. "Tonight I'm bulletproof." Leaning closer, he kissed the spot behind her ear and whispered, "I'm sitting here with the most beautiful woman in the room."

"Quit it. I told you that you don't have to say stuff like that." She squirmed when his fingers slipped too far under the fabric. "Watch it."

"I'm being careful. No one can see."

She supposed that was true. The room was dimly lit to begin with and their little corner darker than most. No wonder he'd been so pleased to nab this booth.

His finger grazed her nipple and she gasped. "Dammit, Gunner."

"We're fine," he murmured.

"You folks about ready for another round?" Cindy, their waitress, was all teeth and very blonde. And acted as if she hadn't seen a thing.

Even if she had, it couldn't have been much. Bar people saw a lot worse as the nights stretched into the wee hours. Mallory could attest to that.

"I'm ready," Gunner said, looking at her.

"No kidding," she muttered, and nodded at Cindy, who smiled and scribbled their order on her way to the next table.

"Hey, I straight-up told you my motives for buying the dress weren't pure."

He moved his hand to her thigh, startling her.

"I should've listened."

His low, sexy laugh almost distracted her from his palm sliding higher up her leg.

"Are you really that horny you can't wait until we get back to the hotel?"

Irritation flared in his eyes. "It has nothing to do with being horny. But if that explanation is easier for you to accept, fine."

"Gunner…" She hated how he'd pulled his hand away and laid his head back, his eyes closing briefly. "I was teasing."

"Were you?"

She paused to think. "Half and half."

"Well, you get credit for honesty." With a small shrug, he picked up his Sam Adams and drained the bottle. "Look, I just wanted you to have something from me, okay?"

She wanted to ask what he'd meant by an "easier explanation" but it felt like something she should already know. Later she'd be able to figure it out on her own, when her brain was less hazy from the beer, from Gunner's nearness, from the thrill of being on her very first real date.

God that sounded so weird, even if it was just in her head.

He was still holding the empty bottle, both hands wrapped around it. Probably an excuse to not touch her. She swept a sideways glance at him. He was facing the stage, eyes forward, his jaw clenched.

"And another thing," he said, turning abruptly to her. "Why is it okay for Dale and Wayne and every other

Tom, Dick and Harry to give you gifts but I get my ass chewed for buying you a lousy dress?"

Mallory blinked at him. Where the hell had that come from?

"Bringing me back a keepsake from someplace exotic that I'll never see is completely different."

"How?"

"Are you serious? Those guys are just— I'm not—" She stopped just in time, silently cursing herself. Jesus, she was not in love with Gunner. And even if she was, and she wasn't, she wouldn't admit it to him.

Her hands started shaking but she took care of that by sitting on them. So Gunner wouldn't see, mostly, but there was also a possibility she might try to strangle him. Why make it too easy?

"Go on," he said. Even with his brows pulled together in a frown he still managed to look mildly amused. "Finish what you were saying."

"No. I changed my mind."

"Chicken."

They stared at each other as several long seconds ticked by. Of course there was no way he'd guessed what she had been about to say. But he should know better than to press her when she was embarrassed.

She unclenched her teeth. "Now who's being a dick?"

His smug grin couldn't be more annoying. "Um, was that an admission of guilt?"

She thought a moment. It might've sounded like it. But did he really have to point it out? She picked up a peanut and threw it at him.

He jerked back so it missed, and laughed.

"I've been having the best night of my whole life and I'm not letting you ruin it, Gunner," she said. "I'm not."

The smirk disappeared. With a look of tenderness that made her chest ache, he put his arm around her. "I'm having a good time, too."

Much as she hated her impulsive outburst, she hadn't exaggerated. Although... She laid a hand on his thigh. "I had two other pretty cool nights," she said softly. "This might make it a three-way tie."

He touched her chin, gently tipping her head back. "I agree," he said and kissed her.

The warmth in her cheeks spread to her body as Gunner's tongue demanded entry. He seemed more rushed than usual, probing deep with raw, hungry strokes that seemed almost desperate to sample every bit of her mouth.

She didn't know she'd moved her hand higher up his leg until she felt the beginning of his erection nudging the back of her fingers. A quiet groan rose from his throat and filled her mouth. In another second she was going to crawl on top of him and forget they were sitting in a crowded bar.

Her eyes fluttered open just in time to see their waitress approaching. Mallory pulled back. "Incoming."

It took him a moment to get it. He just shook his head as Cindy set their beers in front of them. She smiled but didn't linger.

"How about we make this our last one?" Gunner said, picking up his beer. "Then leave after the next set."

"Fine," she said, her attention drawn to a tiny white-haired woman wearing creased jeans and a pink gingham blouse.

Wild Bill's seemed to cater to the thirtysomething crowd so anyone who looked to be pushing eighty stood out.

Mallory watched the woman pick her way through the layers of sawdust and peanut shells in her pointed cowboy boots and walk onto the empty dance floor. She paused, glanced around as if she might be lost, then continued onto the stage and patiently waited for the band to finish tuning up.

Gunner followed her gaze. "This ought to be good," he said. "She's probably going to ask them to play a waltz."

"Be quiet. I think she might be confused."

"Great," he muttered. "She can join the club."

"I heard that," Mallory shot back and tried not to fret as she watched anxiously to see if a band member or anyone else acknowledged the poor woman.

Josiah, the lead singer, who Mallory needed to contact about hiring them, smiled and gave the woman a slight nod.

She glanced around as she had before and walked briskly to the middle of the floor just as the band started playing Billy Ray Cyrus's "Achy Breaky Heart."

It seemed as if people exploded from their tables onto the dance floor. After a few moments of what looked like mass confusion, they all formed into lines and jumped into the rhythm of the song.

It was crazy. And wonderful. And watching them filled Mallory with a giddy joy she'd never before experienced.

She whipped her gaze to Gunner. "Do you know how to line dance?"

"Hell no, and I'm not about to learn, either."

"Gunner?"

"Mallory…"

She smiled at him.

"Forget it." He shook his head and chugged down some beer. "No," he said, finally meeting her eyes again. "I'm not getting up there and making a fool of myself."

Mallory ignored his stubborn frown and waited patiently, tapping her foot along with the beat of the song. When she thought the time was right, she got up and held out her hand.

He stared at it, then looked up into her pleading eyes.

"Goddamn it," he muttered, getting to his feet and taking her hand.

14

GUNNER KEPT HIS cool and waited until the bickering older couple stepped out of the elevator. They couldn't seem to agree on their floor and had stopped the car once already. The door had barely slid closed when he backed Mallory up against the wall and swept his tongue inside her mouth.

"Hey," she said, laughing and still out of breath from the last kiss before they'd been interrupted. "We have only five more floors. You can wait."

He managed a grunt. Working his hands between her and the wall, he cupped her butt and pulled her against him. He was nuts, and too hard to be torturing himself like this.

"See?" Eyes drifting closed, she let her head fall back and he accepted the invitation to kiss her throat. "Line dancing agrees with you."

Pausing briefly, he murmured, "Bullshit," and then went back to kissing the side of her neck, her jaw, her chin, before moving on to lick the hollow above her collarbone.

"Come on," she said with a soft laugh. "You had fun. Admit it."

"I liked being with you and I liked seeing you happy." But suffering through three damn songs? Nowhere close to fun.

"The Full Moon isn't big enough, is it? Maybe buying Fanny was a mistake. Maybe I—"

"Maybe," he said, lifting his head just as she opened her eyes, "you should worry about my fragile ego and quit talking about the bar."

She stared for a moment and then burst out laughing.

"For a bartender you can't hold your liquor worth shit."

Her eyes narrowed. "I didn't drink that much."

He kissed the tip of her nose. "That's my point."

"Look, I'm not even tipsy. I'm just happy, Gunner. Really happy. That's all."

She smiled at him.

He smiled back, but he couldn't help wondering what exactly was making her eyes shine like she'd just cashed in a winning lottery ticket.

Was it because she was starting a new life? Or maybe it was because she was finally having a life, period. Was it possible he had a little something to do with her newfound joy?

He wanted to believe he did, and he knew he'd contributed some, but no sense fooling himself. Mallory didn't think she could count on him when it mattered. She'd proved that when her car had broken down and she'd called Grace.

The toxic mix of anger and disbelief he'd felt when he'd had to hear about it from Ben still got to him.

Jesus, they'd just made love the night before and yet

she'd called Grace and not him. He couldn't seem to get past that.

Hell, it had only happened yesterday, he thought dryly. He'd probably get over it and live.

"What's wrong?" Mallory asked at the same time the elevator dinged.

He stepped aside to let her out first.

"It's the lobby," she said, frowning. "How did we end up back here?"

Yep, it was the lobby all right. Not a soul in sight. It was after 1:30.

No one boarded and the doors closed.

He pushed the button for the twelfth floor and trapped her in the corner, grabbing a handful of her dress. "Let's see if I remember…"

"What are you doing?" she asked, slapping at his hand and giggling.

"What am I doing?" he echoed, moving slowly, enjoying the growing excitement in her sparkling eyes. "Shriek like that again and I'll be sitting in the security office answering a lot of unnecessary questions."

She laughed and turned her face when he tried to kiss her mouth. "We'll miss our floor again…" Her protest trailed off into a breathy moan as he slid a slow hand up her leg.

Smooth as silk and so soft. He felt a shudder ripple through her body. He wanted her so damn much his own hand trembled against her skin.

"Gunner?" she said softly, framing his face with her small hands and waiting for him to look into her eyes. "We're here."

He just nodded and held the door back while he pulled himself out of the fog. She was already waiting in the corridor before he trusted himself to join her. With a sweet smile she slipped her hand in his and they walked in silence to the room.

They each had their own key card but neither of them could find theirs. All Gunner wanted to do was touch the wisps of honey-colored hair curling around Mallory's face. She kept swatting them, and him, away from her cheeks as she searched inside her purse.

He stood there, useless as could be, trying to sort out something he'd thought about earlier. Something that was nagging at him.

And then it registered, nearly clobbering him.

They'd made love.

A few minutes ago his exact thought had been that they'd made love the other night. Not just had sex. A first for him. Because he'd never...

Hell, he wasn't even sure he knew what love really meant.

But Jesus H. Christ. He was pretty damn sure he was in trouble.

MALLORY OPENED THE door with her key card, wishing she knew what was wrong with Gunner. Whatever the problem was it had come on suddenly. She doubted he'd even looked for his key at all. He'd just stood there as though something had hit him upside the head.

"I promise never to keep you out this late again," she said in a teasing tone, hoping to jolt him out of his trance and get him inside the room without making a big deal of it.

He shook his head, chuckling and looking more like himself as he closed the door behind him. "To think I used to be able to party most of the night and make it to the set ready and alert no matter what time they were shooting."

"Ha. You still do." She tossed her purse onto the wing chair. She hated carrying it but the dress had no pockets. "Party, anyway. I wouldn't know if you make it to work on time."

"Where did you get your information? The thrift store?" Pulling her close, he banded his arms around her until not even a sigh could slip between their bodies. "When was the last time I stayed up late partying?"

His gray eyes nearly as dark as midnight, Gunner studied her face with that damn half smile that always gave her a shiver.

Logically, it should've been offset by the sudden surge of heat she felt when his erection pressed against her belly, but all that did was make her weak-kneed. "I don't know specifics."

"So, you don't know, period."

"Probably when you were in Argentina." Oh, hell, why had she brought that up? From the look he was giving her, the same thought occurred to him. "You know what? It was a dumb remark. Forget it."

"I was too busy worrying about unreturned phone calls to be having any fun."

"I know. It was unfair. I'm sorry."

He seemed to be waiting for more detail, but she couldn't go there. Now wasn't the right time to talk about it, if there even was such a thing. His mood had shifted on their second elevator trip. She couldn't pinpoint how or why, but she hadn't imagined it. In fact, he still wasn't quite himself.

But she owed him a truthful explanation. If only

for him to have closure, because that's what he really needed, whether or not he understood that.

She'd finally figured it out, and was ashamed it had taken her so long. The way she'd suddenly disappeared—it was like when her mom had left. Without warning. She'd just packed a bag and hopped on the back of some guy's Harley. Mallory had struggled so hard to understand why. How could it have been that easy to leave her child behind? As if Mallory hadn't meant anything more than the pair of shorts her mom had abandoned because they couldn't fit in her bag.

Mallory had managed to make some peace with it over the years, but sometimes she still had bad days wondering and making up excuses...

Gunner was watching her closely and she drew in a long breath, looking for calm. Who knew what he'd seen in her face? Instead of forcing her to elaborate, he kissed her.

She would tell him. Eventually. Before he left Blackfoot Falls, which was a certainty she couldn't bear to think about. Of course she'd leave out the part about how she might be in love with him. It was too humiliating. For now, it wasn't a crime to simply enjoy each other.

Gunner kept the kiss lazy and G-rated, and it was kind of nice not to be rushed. Though the action in the elevator had been pretty damn hot.

She slid her hand down the front of his jeans, paused to cup him through the denim and reveled in his sharp inhale, in the slow sexy way he moved against her palm.

Using her own hips to keep the fever burning, she went for his buckle.

He broke the kiss but didn't try to stop her. "I'm different now, Mallory," he said, urging her chin up so they could look at each other. "Sure, I might have a beer or a shot with the guys, sometimes even a few drinks after we're done shooting. But I've only been doing that when I'm on location. When we'd shoot around LA, either I went to the Renegade after work, or I was at home sleeping because we knocked off so late." He brushed a stubborn curl away from her eyes. "Didn't you notice?"

"I did," she said slowly, unsure how much she wanted to admit. Like how she'd sometimes driven herself crazy wondering if it was only wishful thinking or if Gunner really was spending more time with her. No, not her personally. That was the kind of daydreaming that got her into trouble. Even now, he'd just mentioned the Renegade. Not her.

"Why did you think I was hanging around so much?" His voice was casual. His arms had loosened around her, and his body was more relaxed. And for the first time that she could remember, he made no effort to hide his thoughts. He let her see how deeply invested he was in her answer.

And it scared the hell out of her.

God, how tempted she was to finish unbuckling him, pull off his jeans, distract him with sex. To do anything to ensure tonight wouldn't be ruined.

Gunner took the decision out of her hands. He kissed her again. Hard. Leaving no room for doubt that he was staking his claim. She wound her arms around his neck as his tongue stroked hers, swept along her teeth, brushed the roof of her mouth, plunged deeper. He seemed to be on a mission to leave nothing untouched.

The more he kissed her, the more she wanted. He kissed her harder and deeper and she wanted even more.

Her muscles quivered with longing and the rest of her body felt close to meltdown.

She rubbed against his erection until he groaned and scooped her up into his strong arms.

She held on tight as he carried her to the bed. But instead of laying her down he left her standing on wobbly legs as he scattered kisses across her throat, down the side of her neck. When she swayed, he tightened an arm around her waist.

"Tell me what you want, baby," he whispered, his breath warm and moist and seductive. "Anything you want."

You.

What if she just went ahead and said it out loud? What was the worst that could happen? He was going to leave no matter what. Go back to his life in LA. Anyway, he'd probably think she only meant sex.

"Everything," she said finally. He could do whatever he wanted with that.

He smiled and pressed his mouth to her throat. Mallory's heart pounded faster with each long slow stroke of his tongue down the slope of her neck. When he got to the strap of her dress, he caught it with his teeth and drew it off her shoulder. His free hand slid along the curve of her backside, squeezing gently.

She clung to him, digging into taut skin and hard muscle, praying he wouldn't release her. Her body was already limp, her legs unsteady. As he worked the strap down her arm, every random scrape of his teeth made her knees even weaker. A few more inches was all it would take to bare her breast to his mouth...

If only he'd hurry.

He pulled up her dress and stripped down her panties before she knew what he was doing. The unexpected move knocked the wind out of her. She swayed to the side but Gunner caught her, wrapping her in his arms and then laying her across the bed.

His hand felt rough and hot on her skin as he pushed the dress up to her waist. Resting his palm on her belly, he paused to take in what he'd uncovered, his mouth curving in a satisfied smile. As his gaze moved over her, fire blazed in his eyes. His fingers lightly brushed the sensitive skin at the top of her sex, before he lifted her left leg and kissed the inside of her knee.

He worked his way down her calf to her ankle, using his lips and tongue, then retraced the moist trail until he reached the inner flesh of her thigh.

"Ah, Mallory," he murmured between slow, damp kisses. "I've wanted this all night." The hushed richness of his hypnotic baritone soothed even as it excited her. "I've wanted *you*. I always want you."

His voice had barely risen to a whisper as he raised his head slightly to meet her gaze. In his eyes, mixed in with the raging want, was a tenderness that tugged at her heart.

She touched his face, then moved her hand to his hair. Burying her fingers in the thick softness, she cupped the back of his head and urged him down and pressed her lips to his mouth. The warm smell of his skin, the smooth firmness of his lips, they filled her senses.

"Your clothes, Gunner," she whispered. "Take them off…"

With slow reluctance, he straightened away from her and unsnapped his shirt, his eyes on her the whole time. His buckle was undone and he got rid of the belt, flinging it aside with the shirt, then pulled off his boots.

Fighting her sudden lethargy, she refused to allow her heavy lids to close. She wanted to watch him, study the dusting of hair across his tanned chest, the ridges of muscle that defined his flat belly.

Every part of her woke up when he got on the bed. "Wait," she said, her voice rising. "Your jeans."

Gunner smiled. "Shh, baby, I'll get to it," he said, and rubbed a soothing hand up her calf as he moved in between her thighs.

He leaned down to kiss her as he grabbed a pillow and tucked it under her head. She saw then he wasn't all that steady himself. He spread her thighs wider and his mouth sank down on her.

The amazing feel of his tongue slipping past her lips stole her breath. His muffled moan sent heat searing through her veins. Whimpering, she caught a fistful of his hair but that didn't stop him. It seemed to excite him.

His pointed tongue probed deep while his finger slipped around her sensitive flesh. He lingered on her clit while she writhed and inhaled great gulps of air that weren't enough.

He sucked hard, blew lightly and licked her with his long flat tongue.

She arched against his mouth, soaring nearer and nearer to orgasm. It was too soon. She wanted it to last. Just a while longer...

The first glimmer of sensation flared in warning. Mallory couldn't have held out if she'd wanted to. She gasped, moaned, whimpered. No matter how hard she bucked, Gunner's mouth stayed on her, ruthlessly pushing her to the next level, his tongue and warm breath fanning the flames that threatened to consume her.

Her heart pounded wildly, her skin tingled and the rest of her soared.

Everything blurred after that, as though she'd lost a measure of time. Vaguely aware that he was now sitting next to her, she blinked at the hand he offered.

He helped her into a sitting position, then tugged her dress up and over her head.

"Be careful," she said, catching his arm as he was about to toss it. A small self-conscious laugh escaped her. "I love my dress. Thank you." She put her arms around him, and rubbed her beaded nipples against his back. "You're probably sick of seeing me in jeans."

"That's not why I bought it," he said, his voice gruff as he twisted around and sucked a nipple into his mouth.

He tried urging her to lie back but she wasn't about to let him have his way. It was her turn.

"I want to be on top."

He sucked harder, and she shuddered.

"Fine by me," he said and she jumped in to help him undress.

With his belt gone, it was easy to undo the top button of his jeans, but getting the zipper down was something else. He ended up doing that part, but she tugged the jeans down, along with his very sexy boxer briefs.

But now, she wanted him on his back. With a flat palm to his chest, his heart pounding hard and fast against her hand, she pushed him back, skittering away so he could bring his legs up.

He adjusted the pillow as she got ready, making sure he was in a position to watch.

When she didn't immediately climb on board, he frowned. "What are you waiting for?"

"Shh, baby," she mimicked, teasing him by dragging

the tips of her fingernails up the inside of his thigh. "I'll get to it."

He narrowed his darkened eyes and gave in to a smile.

She straddled his thighs and he jerked his hips up to meet her. "Easy, cowboy," she whispered, thrumming with excitement and not sure how long she could play this out.

Finally, she raised herself over him.

She started her very slow descent and the moan he let out thrilled her to her toes. To think she could make Gunner putty was almost unbelievable, although she wasn't far behind. She sank down another inch and tightened her inner muscles, squeezing as hard as she could.

Gunner's head went back into the pillow, his jaw clenched, his groan deep and raw, rumbling from way down in his throat.

He grasped her hips, trying to control her movements. But she wasn't ready to sink all the way down yet and wouldn't be hurried.

He surged up.

She was breathless for a moment, startled by the unexpected impact. What started out as a soft gasp morphed into a whimper at the sensation of being utterly and completely filled until she thought she might explode. Every muscle in his body was like steel, tense and straining, his fingers digging into her hips. Mallory had the vague thought that it just might be the only thing keeping her intact.

She gave up any illusion of control. Neither of them fought the rhythm that came as naturally as it would have if they'd done this a thousand times. They wouldn't last very long. She knew that, and yet when the first wave overtook her, she gasped, completely unprepared. Her reflexive arch pulled him deeper inside her. Each spasm robbed her of more air.

Gunner moaned, a harsh, rough cry that sounded as if it had come from someplace so deep and primal it had never existed before this moment. His possessive grip on her hips tightened as he thrust up past the hard clench of muscle convulsing around him. His final moan could've woken the dead.

By the time they'd both settled, she didn't have a bone left in her body. But she still managed to smile when he wrapped himself around her like the most wonderful blanket ever.

Oh, yeah. She didn't have it bad at all.

15

GUNNER KEPT HIS attention on the road in front of them, clenching and unclenching his teeth, wondering how the hell everything had gone south so damn quickly.

Mallory's arms were crossed as she stared out her window. They were only fifteen minutes from Blackfoot Falls. Thank God. It seemed she was getting grumpier by the mile.

Man, had she been pissed when he'd admitted there was nothing wrong with her car. She'd just run out of gas. It was good news, for fuck sake. She should be thrilled she wouldn't be stuck with a huge repair bill. Although he had a feeling most of her anger was aimed at herself for overlooking the fuel gauge. Which she said was his fault because *he'd been distracting her*. He figured that was a good thing but he kept his opinion to himself.

Anything he'd said so far had just given her more ammunition. Even when he'd explained that the Hyundai hadn't stayed on the side of the highway for long. Instead of being relieved the car was already gassed up and sitting in front of her house, she got pissed all over again.

What if someone had found the key he'd left under the mat and had stolen it? What if Billy, the kid who worked for Ben—and who Gunner now owed fifty bucks—had decided to go for a joyride?

Pointing out that neither of those two things had happened had only made her madder. So he left out the obvious fact that no one in their right mind would steal that piece of shit. And a joyride? In that? Come on.

All he'd wanted to do was prove that she could count on him, and this was what he got.

"What did you tell Ben?" she asked, her arms still crossed. "Does he know you were with me?"

"I didn't tell him anything but I'm sure he suspects."

"Why?"

"Why? From the other night when I stayed over with you." Gunner knew they'd agreed to keep their arrangement quiet, which he would've done anyway. But Ben wasn't stupid. "He knew I didn't make it back to the ranch until the next day. Who else would I have spent the night with?"

She laughed, shrugged. "Just about anyone."

Now that pissed *him* off. "You know, Mallory, I probably deserved that crack at some point in my life, but not now." In his younger days he might have been less discriminating and not always discreet. But he'd never been the kind to go sniffing around for the hell of it.

"I'm sorry," she said. "I didn't mean that the way it sounded."

He wasn't a hundred percent sure he believed that, but he was willing to give her the benefit of the doubt. Especially after last night. The hotel, dinner, her in that dress… Everything had gone so smoothly it had given him hope. Made him think that if Ben could be serious about wanting a partner, maybe it was time for Gunner to give some thought to his future. No, he'd never cared for small-town living, but he was older now, and being here with Mallory would be worth it.

Briefly taking his eyes off the road, he glanced at her. "Besides, why would I be with anyone else when I have you?" he said, and reached for her hand.

As she entwined her fingers with his, her lips lifted in a small smile. "Do you think Ben will stick it out here?"

"You mean ranching?"

She nodded.

"Have you seen the Silver Spur? He's put a lot of sweat and money into the place. It's really something."

"I know. They had me out there for dinner. It's just…" She shrugged. "I mean, he's his own boss and he loves working with horses, but there can't be much excitement in running a ranch."

Gunner tensed. "I don't think that's what he's looking for."

"Maybe not, but what happens in a few years when he's bored and restless? Stuntmen are a whole different kind of animal," she said, with the casual conviction of someone who didn't allow for the possibility of being wrong. "Of course I don't have to tell you. I mean, stuntmen aren't exactly known for leading tame lives. It's all about risk, excitement, adventure…"

"That's true for some of them," he said calmly. "Not all. It might be a rush in the beginning but that doesn't last forever."

"Retirement? They don't know the meaning of the word. They have to be booted out or injured before they quit. And even then they can't make peace with sitting on the sidelines."

He wasn't sure she'd even heard what he'd said. They hadn't gotten much sleep. The whole thing about the car had upset her. Or maybe he just sucked at this relationship business and didn't know when to zone out. Let her talk. Pretend he was listening. Hell, he didn't know.

"Take my father," she said and pulled her hand away to rearrange her ponytail. "A perfect example. After the accident, he got enough money to open the Renegade. Owning a bar was what he wanted. At least that's what he'd say. But he wasn't happy. He'd get drunk and moan about how much life sucked. How he'd been cheated. How stunt work was the only thing he'd ever cared about. I was a kid, *his* kid, sitting right there, listening to him."

On a deep breath, she turned her head to look out her window.

Yeah, she'd been hurt by the old man, by both her parents. Gunner wouldn't argue that. He'd heard Coop go off on his self-pity rants many times. But Gunner was still offended. "I liked your dad okay, but with all due respect, Mallory, don't ever compare me to him again."

Her gaze flew back to him. He kept his on the highway, but from the corner of his eye he saw that she was staring. She hadn't returned her hand to his, and he hadn't reached for it, either.

"I wasn't. Really," she said. "You aren't anything like him. I know that. I'm sorry that it came out wrong."

"Coop was a shitty father, but that had nothing to do with him being a stuntman. Ben, me, a lot of guys, we don't all live for the job. At first, yeah, probably. And then one day you realize it's the only thing you know how to do and the money is too good to just walk away. At least not without a damn good plan."

Silence lasted long enough for him to regret including

himself in the mix. That opened him up for questions. And now sure as hell wasn't the time to discuss the possibility of him turning his life upside down on a gamble. There were still too many considerations.

"You're not tired of stunt work," she said.

Well, it wasn't a question. Despite his irritation, he almost laughed. Guess she had all the answers.

"Are you?"

He saw a sign up ahead. His eyes were too weary to make out the words, but he knew it meant they were close to town. Good. This dialogue was headed for trouble. "Getting there," he said finally.

"Since when?"

"For a while."

She fidgeted, then he heard her quietly clear her throat. "Have you decided on when you'll be leaving?"

He slid her an amused look. "Trying to get rid of me?"

"Of course not." She studied him for a moment. "I hope you were kidding," she said, sounding cross. "I only asked because you rarely take time off. You always have work. Dale and Lawson are jealous as hell that every stunt coordinator in the business has you on speed dial."

Gunner shook his head. "Lawson's a wimp. He's turned down enough of the tougher shit that all the big guns have quit asking for him. I don't know what Dale's problem is."

Great. Now they were both in crappy moods.

Her phone signaled she had a text. She dug it out of her pocket. "Oh. Okay. Sadie confirmed the water main is fixed and I can open tonight."

"You don't sound thrilled."

"I wouldn't have minded staying closed. I'm pretty tired."

"So do it. You're the boss."

"I don't know. Elaine's already lost a day's work. She might need the money." Mallory thumped her head back against the headrest. "What am I saying? *I* need the money."

He'd been wondering how she was doing financially and if he could help. He wouldn't ask now.

They entered the town limits and drove past the crew that had been working on the water main.

"They look thirsty. Could be your first customers," Gunner said, just to say something that wasn't going to blow up in their faces.

Mallory ignored the comment and they rode in silence down Main to her street.

He parked behind her car and waited for her to say something snarky.

"So," she said, picking up her dress and carefully draping it over her arm, "I guess you're not going to tell me when you're heading back to LA."

"If I knew I'd tell you."

"Fine." She opened her door and paused. He thought she might invite him inside. Instead she nodded at the Hyundai. "What do I owe you?"

"Nothing."

"Bull. I know you have to pay the kid for the gas and his time."

"Jesus, Mallory, don't worry about it."

"I want a number, Gunner. I mean it. And I should pay for the hotel, too. You wouldn't have gone to Kalispell if it weren't for me—"

"You really want to piss me off, huh?" He could feel his temper fraying.

"I'm not saying we have to settle up at this minute," she said, that stubborn streak of hers refusing to let her back off. "Anyway, thanks." She climbed out of the truck. "For everything."

So much for a goodbye kiss. Maybe she'd like to shake hands.

"Listen," he said, keeping his cool. She had a long night ahead of her, and he didn't want to be a jerk. "If you need—"

"Nope. I'm fine," she said and closed the door.

Gunner stared in disbelief as she opened the gate to her walkway without so much as a backward glance. She'd cut him off. Hadn't even known what he was going to say. What the hell was that about?

He leaned across the seat and opened the passenger door. "Hey, Mallory." She didn't turn around right away, but he waited until she did. "Say the word and I'm out of here, sweetheart. I'm sure you won't have trouble finding some other guy to help paint that nice little picket fence of yours."

The words tasted bitter on his tongue, but he was too damn angry to smooth them over. Her running hot and cold like this was bullshit. He'd driven fourteen hundred miles chasing after her, trying to see if they could work things out. And he was sick of being the only one making the effort.

The second she spun back around and hurried up the porch steps, he slammed the truck door and sped away.

MALLORY GOT TO the bar ten minutes late. She felt like crap when she saw Elaine standing near the door in a small wedge of shade, fanning herself.

"I'm so sorry," she said, trying to insert the key and missing until her third attempt.

"Slow down, honey. I'm not going anywhere and neither is that lock."

"I'd like you to have a key," Mallory told her as they walked inside where it was at least a thousand degrees cooler. "If you don't want the responsibility, that's fine. I totally understand. So think about it. And let me know."

"I don't have to think. Makes sense. So as long as you trust me, sure, I'll keep a key."

"Why wouldn't I trust you?"

"Well, you've known me less than two weeks. I thought you California people were more guarded than that."

Mallory laughed. It was either that or start crying.

"Are you okay?" Elaine was setting out mugs and frowning. "You don't look so good."

"I'm fine. Late night."

"Ah." Elaine smiled. "Gunner?"

"Why would you think—" Mallory sighed. She was too tired to lie or pretend or even be human. Just as long as no more tears fell she'd be okay.

The waterworks had started earlier, halfway to her front door, but she was fairly certain Gunner wasn't the wiser.

"I think we're going to be busy tonight," Elaine said. "Any chance you read the manual so we can plug in Fanny?"

"Um, no." Of course she should have, instead of screwing around in Kalispell. "Sorry."

"No need to apologize. It's your bar." Elaine glanced at her watch. "Want me to give it a look if I have time?"

Mallory had to think a moment. Right. The instructions were in the cabinet under the register. She laid them on the bar.

"So, you think we'll be busy?"

"You must've heard about the movie being shot in the area," she said, and Mallory nodded. "Yesterday they made camp about twenty miles south of here and we're the closest town."

"Oh, believe me, they've brought plenty of booze with them. But when they get tired of hanging out at their trailers, we should get some business out of it."

She glanced over at Fanny's instructions. They probably weren't difficult to understand, but it was better to let Elaine read them. Mallory's concentration was shaky at best. Her thoughts kept jumping back to Gunner and the stupid things they'd said to each other and how everything had gotten blown out of proportion.

God, she'd run out of gas? How humiliating. She'd never done anything like that before. Being consumed with thoughts of Gunner, daring to dream about a future with him, was making her sloppy. She'd end up no better here in Blackfoot Falls if she didn't pull herself together. Sex while he was here was fine. But that's all it could be.

Part of her knew he'd only tried to be helpful, taking care of her car and giving her a night on the town. But he should've kept her informed. She had to make her own decisions concerning the bar, her car, her life in general.

Didn't he realize the moment he left she'd be completely on her own again? Sure, there was Ben, and Mallory was getting to know Grace and Elaine and Sadie. Luckily she liked them and they seemed to like her. If an emergency arose, she knew she could call any one of them and they'd gladly help if they were able.

But the regular everyday stuff fell to her. Even the little things she'd gotten in the habit of bouncing off him. Gunner was making it tougher to say goodbye. She had to explain it to him, make him understand she wasn't trying to get rid of him. Or hoping to snare some cowboy into filling his shoes.

That last remark of his still pissed her off. But that was okay. In fact, it was her saving grace. Remembering it helped keep the tears at bay.

"Oh, I almost forgot. I ran into Cecil at the Food Mart." Elaine brought out the bowl of limes and smiled at Mallory's blank look. "The electrician?"

"Right."

"He has two days open if you want him to work on the stage. I think you have his number."

Mallory nodded. "I was going to tell you, I heard Boot Stompin' last night. They're really good."

"Yeah, that's what my neighbor said. They're new and kinda young, aren't they?"

"That's the only reason I can afford them." She'd exchanged info with their lead singer last night and had received a text from him an hour ago. "I can get them for Fridays for sure."

"Hey, a weekend night? That's pretty good."

"I think so, too." She would've asked Gunner what he thought, but not now. Probably not even later. Unless he surprised her and showed up tonight. Which was doubtful. They'd both been so angry.

And exhausted. Hopefully their harsh words would lose some of the sting and blow over after they both got some rest. Or maybe his solution would be to leave tomorrow.

God, the thought depressed her.

Did he really believe she was anxious for him to leave?

That's not what she wanted. It was the complete opposite. And he hadn't helped by pretending he was tired of stunt work. Had he thought that's what she wanted to hear? She wasn't as good at hiding her emotions as Gunner. She'd fallen hard for him, and all these new raw feelings inside her weren't easy to ignore. Had she given herself away and scared him?

Damn, she wished she could replay their last ten minutes together in slow motion. Just so she could get a grip on what was real versus what she might have imagined in his face, his tone. Everything seemed fuzzy.

Okay, maybe he was getting tired of the work, although she found it odd he'd never mentioned it before. The thing was, it wouldn't last. She knew Gunner. He liked doing risky stunts and being in the action. He didn't want a slow, uneventful life.

And she did.

16

FRIDAY NIGHT WAS one of those nights when Mallory wondered if she'd taken on more than she could handle. The Full Moon was packed. It seemed everyone wanted to ride Fanny, she obviously needed to buy another pool table, and if one more person asked for the darts, she was liable to throw them out on their ass. For God's sake, she'd put a sign right there on the dartboard that read Not Tonight.

Elaine had the good sense to consider that with this many people darts meant nothing but trouble.

Oh, and it would've been really helpful had Mallory remembered to order more beer and tequila for the weekend. If she ran out, she didn't know what she would do. Certainly not trouble Sadie. After all her kindness, it bothered Mallory to hear the Watering Hole had been dead all week.

It was almost 10:00 and Elaine and Heather had been hustling since the doors opened. Sheila had pitched in, though she wasn't on the schedule and had to leave early. Even the dance floor was crowded with couples moving to the jukebox music. Maybe hiring a band was an unnecessary expense. Mallory would have to ask Gunner what he...

Knocking over the rum and Coke she'd just poured, she bit off a curse. Mallory had been like this since she'd opened. Clumsy, quick to snap, on the verge of tears.

She hadn't expected to see him last night. It would have been too soon and he'd probably crashed early, anyway. But she thought she might've heard from him by now. Or hoped he'd at least drop by.

It was up to her. She'd have to be the one to make the next move. Which just felt right. The moment she had a second she'd call him. Or maybe a text was better.

No. Definitely a call.

The door opened and Sadie walked in with some people Mallory didn't know. Sadie was laughing so maybe she didn't hate Mallory's guts for stealing her customers. She smiled at the group and recognized Rachel, who she'd met at the diner last week while they waited for cinnamon rolls.

"Well, gee, now I know why my place looks like a funeral parlor," Sadie said, leaning an elbow on the bar and glancing around the room.

Mallory winced. "It's just because we're new."

"I know that. I'm just teasing you. In fact, I brought you more customers." She nodded at a pair of tall, good-looking men. "Cole and Jesse McAllister, say hi to Mallory, our new barkeep."

"Oh, you're Rachel's brothers," she said. "Nice to meet you."

Jesse smiled. "Same here."

His brother nodded, then glanced back to where Rachel and a blonde woman had stopped to talk. "I remember the days when people used to associate us with the Sundance. And now it's 'So you're Rachel's brothers.'"

Sadie chuckled. "Well, she is a pistol, that one. The woman lollygagging with her is Cole's wife, Jamie. Don't know if you've met her yet."

Mallory shook her head, then looked past the blonde when the front door opened and a man entered. At first glimpse she thought he was Gunner and her heart slid down to her stomach.

Cole turned briefly. "That was fast. Matt's here," he said. "He's Rachel's husband."

Worried that she'd given him the wrong impression, Mallory said, "I have a friend who's visiting. He kind of reminds me of him. I had to look twice."

"Gunner?" Jesse asked, and without waiting for a reply glanced back. "Yeah, I can see it."

Heather put a ticket directly in front of Mallory and she got to work pouring two tequila sunrises. "What can I get you all?"

"Beer for us," Cole said, then looked at his brother. "He's the guy checking out Ben's operation, right?"

Jesse nodded. "I think they used to work together. Didn't Gunner do stunt work?"

"He still does," Mallory said, her mind circling. Odd way to put it—*checking out Ben's operation*.

"Hey, guys," Elaine greeted the brothers, then sidled up to Mallory. "Sorry, but I really need those drinks," she said under her breath and set down two more tickets.

Mallory just nodded and kept working. No time to be thinking about Gunner.

"Is that for little Kyle Higgins?" Sadie asked, squinting at the collection jar beside the register. "You should bring it up here so folks will notice it."

The moment Cole and Jesse saw it they dug into their pockets and pulled out money. So did three other men sitting at the bar. Elaine had asked to set it out for a seven-year-old who needed surgery—his family had no health insurance. She'd explained it was common practice for businesses to collect donations.

Mallory was so touched she'd pledged to contribute a quarter for every drink or beer she sold for the whole week. She did as Sadie suggested and moved the jar.

Amazing how many customers began stuffing it with bills. It was almost too much for Mallory in her ridiculous emotional state. She wasn't even sure why she felt weepy, except that it had something to do with Gunner and the mess she'd gotten herself into.

Rachel, her husband and Cole's wife were headed toward them when Jamie saw a table being vacated and grabbed it. Sadie shooed the men over and got behind the bar with Mallory.

So did Rachel. "What can we do?"

Sadie didn't wait for an answer but started filling pitchers.

"You guys don't have to—"

The women cut her off with loud matching laughs. "Really?" Rachel said. "You think you're gonna get rid of us?"

"Okay, so I have to hire more people," Mallory muttered, embarrassed. "Though not if I keep putting customers to work."

Sadie gave her a motherly pat that made her want to cry. "You have Sheila working on call. That's enough for now. It won't be like this all the time." The older woman studied her for a moment. "Go take ten minutes. We've got this."

Mallory had no choice. She couldn't trust herself not to start sobbing in front of everyone.

She slipped out the back where the stinky Dumpster was located. No one would bother her back here. She found a spot upwind and dug out her phone. All she could do was stare at it for a minute. She wanted to call, hear Gunner's voice, but she really didn't have time to talk to him. And she wasn't completely certain she'd be able to without falling apart.

A text was perfect. It would help her get her mind off him. Maybe. At least she'd get to say she was sorry. If he wasn't still angry, they could talk later.

I'm sorry. About everything.

She stared at the words, wondering if she should add that she missed him. No. This was enough for now.

Maybe forever.

Not a helpful thought. She hit Send before she added something stupid then checked the time. She'd only been gone for three minutes so she ducked into the rest-room—and wished she hadn't looked at herself in the mirror. Bloodshot eyes, pasty skin. Even her lips were pale. No wonder Sadie had chased her out.

Instead of running home and hiding under the covers like she wanted to do, Mallory returned to her post and got busy. She felt better having apologized, even if it was with a text. At least she'd made the first move. In fact, she ended up shooing Rachel and Sadie out from behind the bar and sent them with free drinks to their table.

Two minutes later Sadie returned. "I meant to tell you that your friend Gunner was here. When you were taking your break."

Mallory's jaw nearly hit the floor. "What did he say?"

"Nothing. Walked in, stayed by the door, looked around and left." Sadie shrugged. "I figured I'd tell you anyway." She started to turn and paused to wag a finger. "Quit giving away drinks." Her face softened. "Elaine told me what you're doing for the Higgins boy. That's real nice. But free drinks on top of that? Uh-uh."

"Elaine has a big mouth," Mallory muttered, although it was hard to think about anything but Gunner. She waited until Sadie was back at the table before checking her phone.

Me too. Plans tomorrow?

She smiled so hard her cheeks cramped.

Oh, yeah. She had plans all right. To screw his brains out. Just let him try to talk her out of it.

GUNNER HAD BARELY pulled to the curb and Mallory was already on her porch, closing the door behind her. He got out of the truck and jumped over her gate.

"What are you doing?" She stopped in the middle of her walkway, staring at him with a dazed smile. "I thought we were going to Safe Haven."

At the last second he remembered he was wearing his hat. He yanked it off and swept her into his arms. Startled, she blinked at him and giggled until he kissed her silent.

She tasted minty and comforting as she welcomed him inside her sweet, eager mouth, and for the first time in forty-eight hours, he began to relax. He couldn't figure out how that was possible, when his heart was racing like a thoroughbred smelling victory. Lately it seemed Mallory was having that effect on him more and more.

And when she wound her arms tighter around his neck and buried her fingers deeper into his hair, it took every shred of willpower not to carry her inside and make love to her for a week.

Her soft whimper did it. Gave him that slight push toward the edge. Another few seconds and they wouldn't make it past the porch.

Painful as it was, he broke the kiss.

She stared at him with glazed eyes. "Was that just in case the neighbors were wondering?"

"Something like that." He settled his hat on his head, though maybe he should use it to hide his erection. "Ready?"

"You certainly are." Her cheeky smile faltered as she lifted her gaze to his.

"Get in the truck, sweetheart, or face the consequences."

Mallory hesitated, her eyes turning that dark sexy shade of green. "Doesn't sound like such a bad thing…"

Heat and need surged through him. "We can skip Safe Haven."

"Are they expecting you?"

"I can reschedule." He watched her moisten her lips, knowing she was tempted but uncertain. He moved closer to help tip the scale.

She stepped back. "Let's get it over with. You said we'd be about two hours, right?"

Oh, hell.

Nah, sticking to the plan was better in the long run. He'd been doing a lot of thinking and he had to show her that this thing between them wasn't just about sex.

It wouldn't be easy. Especially considering her bias toward stuntmen. But he figured quitting Hollywood and moving to Blackfoot Falls would show her that he was dead serious.

He'd already talked to Ben, who was enthusiastic about making Gunner a partner. They'd discussed buy-in money, expansion plans and the role Gunner would play if he signed on. It wasn't set in stone yet, but the option was there.

"You're a tease," he said and opened the truck door for her.

She made a smart remark and he swatted her bottom just before she slid onto the seat.

Casual touching had turned into something different and he didn't know when that had happened. As if he needed one more thing to analyze. Jesus. He'd end up a candidate for sainthood by the time this proving himself business was all over.

The ride to the large animal sanctuary lasted somewhere around thirty minutes. He kept his hands on the wheel for most of it, but gave in and held her hand a couple of times. They talked about everything from the dark clouds coming from the Rockies and moving toward them to the miniseries and indie film being shot nearby, and what sort of business it could mean for the Full Moon.

Mallory seemed surprised that he had no interest in going out to the set, and he used the opportunity to subtly reinforce his readiness to leave stunt work and move on.

Safe Haven was off the beaten path but easy to find. Gunner parked next to an old white pickup loaded with bales of hay and chicken wire. The sanctuary appeared to be a mix of old, new and refurbished with barns, sheds, a recently constructed log house and two brand-new-looking stables. Lots of corrals filled with mustangs and just about every other kind of horse. Had to be at least fifty of them penned up between the barn and stable.

"What do they mean by large animals?" Mallory asked once they'd both climbed out of the truck. "No dogs or cats?"

"Mostly they take in abandoned horses and cows from what I understand." He nodded toward an older woman emerging from the barn, followed by a white pygmy goat. "Here comes someone who could probably answer your question."

Mallory gasped with delight. "Is that a goat? How cute is that?"

"Gunner?" the woman said, her hand extended before he nodded. "I'm Kathy. We spoke on the phone." She had some grip for someone small and wiry and pushing sixty.

"Thanks for meeting with us," he said. "This is Mallory."

Kathy smiled and then grunted when the goat head-butted her from behind. "Okay, okay," she muttered, turning to the animal. "This is Pinocchio, chief troublemaker."

Mallory was all smiles. "May I pet him?"

"Sure you can," Kathy said and stepped aside. "Now, he may play hard to get at first. On the flip side, if he takes a cotton to you, he could follow you around until you leave."

Mallory put out a tentative hand. The goat moved forward and she jerked back.

Grinning, Gunner slid an arm around her. "We have

a city girl here," he told Kathy, who'd figured that out for herself and was smiling. "Go ahead, sweetheart, he won't hurt you."

"He has horns," Mallory said, frowning with uncertainty. "I'll wait till later. See if he likes me first."

With a laugh, Kathy turned to Gunner. "You're mainly interested in mustangs, is that right?"

"For the most part." Gunner tugged his hat rim down to block the sun's glare and nodded at the corral where a young man was fixing a railing. "But those are some fine-looking palominos. The black, too. I wouldn't mind a closer look."

"You've got a good eye. We just got them a week ago so Ben hasn't seen them yet. Poor guy's been running ragged. I'm glad he finally has someone working with him."

Mallory turned sharply to look at him. He avoided her eyes and focused only on the palominos.

"So, are you the head honcho here?" Gunner asked.

"Only temporarily," Kathy said as they started to walk. "My husband, Levi, and I have volunteered here for years. Same as many of the folks you might see milling about. Levi and Chuck are in the quarantine stable right now. Volunteers help keep this place going. Shea McAllister and I are filling in until the board finds a new director. The pay is terrible but that cute little log house comes with the job. Either of you interested?" Her grin was aimed at Mallory.

She just laughed. "Um, yeah…that's not gonna happen."

"My husband and I considered it but we want to move closer to our grandkids," Kathy said just as a cloud passed over the sun, and she stopped to look up at the increasingly overcast sky. "I was hoping those clouds wouldn't come east for a while."

"I figured you'd be praying for rain."

"Yep, we need some of that for sure." She pulled a walkie-talkie out of the back pocket of her jeans. "I'm worried about the high school kids working in the alfalfa field. I don't need them getting the four-wheelers and tractor stuck in the mud."

While Kathy tried to reach the kids, Gunner watched Mallory warily eye the goat. Pinocchio seemed equally interested in her. Gunner didn't think the animal was up to mischief but Mallory wasn't taking any chances.

He waited for one of them to make their move but then got distracted by a handsome silver stallion being led toward the corral.

Pale-colored horses seldom caught his attention. But this guy, with his silver mane and tail, his head high and proud, was a beauty.

"Where the heck are those darn kids?" Kathy muttered and shook the walkie-talkie. "I sure wish we had better luck with cell phones out here."

Gunner could hear the static from where he stood several feet away. The sun was still hidden. He felt the first few drops of rain hit his arm and looked up. They were in for a downpour for sure.

"Oh, well, I guess I'll have to trust they have enough sense to come back before it gets too muddy."

Kathy's words were punctuated by an earsplitting clap of thunder. She and Mallory both jumped. The silver stallion reared up. Whinnies came from the corralled horses as they moved restlessly against the rails.

Lightning came quick and from not far away as another window-rattling thunderclap made everyone duck.

Gunner could hear the agitation of the horses, and he felt torn between getting Mallory inside and running over to help in the large corral.

His decision was made for him. The kid who'd been fixing the railing jumped over the logs in the nick of time, just avoiding being crushed when the terrified animals broke through the fence. They were too crowded and too scared to stay where they were, and they knew to run like hell when the skies got mean.

Kathy was moving now, toward the corral and the young man, fast as she could, and Gunner hoped she didn't think she was going to hold back twenty-some mustangs. But her voice carried over a stretch of silence. "...the kids! I can't reach 'em."

He remembered. Teenagers with ATVs and a stampede was a disaster waiting to happen. "Mallory," he yelled over another boom, "get inside."

"What are you—"

He was running, and he couldn't spare her an answer or it could be too late. The silver horse was the closest, and at least he had a bridle. Gunner pulled the reins from the boy's hands, grabbed on to the silver's mane and swung up. The stallion wasn't happy, but Gunner tightened his thighs around the horse's withers.

Once he was situated, Kathy must have understood exactly what he was doing because she stopped waving her walkie-talkie. "They're in the alfalfa field," she yelled. Then she pointed north.

The rains let loose as Gunner leaned forward. Silver bolted, the next clap of thunder working like a starter pistol.

Gunner only let go of the mane to jam his hat down harder, and then it was like flying through a damn car wash. Every ounce of his concentration was on his balance and learning Silver in the worst possible conditions. One misstep could be costly, and there were no wranglers around to safety check this stunt.

But those kids. If they started up those ATVs when the herd approached them, someone was bound to get hurt.

There was no use going after the mustangs, although he doubted teenage boys would stop to think things through. But if Gunner was lucky, he might be able to get all the kids back safely.

He was already so wet it was like standing in the shower with his clothes on. But damn if Silver wasn't a firecracker. His gait was smooth as silk even through the torrent. If this horse wasn't spoken for…

Shit.

The mustangs were just up ahead. Right at the alfalfa field.

Gunner urged Silver to go faster and the stallion reacted with a fierce surge forward. It was all Gunner could do to stay on top of him.

He veered right to get outside the herd, to tell the idiots on the ATVs to turn off the motors, stand down and be still.

Christ, one of them started waving his hat like some kind of rodeo clown. Then another kid followed suit, and Gunner's plan was pretty much shot to shit. There was only one thing to do.

He ran straight up the middle, through the pack. Almost got ripped off the stallion by a crazed gray, but he got the kicking horse to run away from the boys instead of over them.

The horse weighed at least seven hundred pounds,

and spooked? It could do some real damage to anything in its path. Luckily, the other group of kids froze as he approached. Good reaction. The only safe one.

But there were more kids on the other two ATVs, and they were doubled up, and moving.

Gunner timed his shift to the left so he didn't smack into a dun, then he went straight toward the boys. "Shut off the motors!" He'd never yelled so loud. Probably end up with a torn larynx. "Keep still. Stop waving your goddamned hats!"

At least the kids on the nearest four-wheeler heard him, and they stopped what they were doing. Gunner sidled up to the next one, yelling for all he was worth.

Under him, Silver worked like an old friend. The last ATV shut down and finally, all the kids were standing as still as statues as the mustangs weaved their way through to freedom.

At least it wasn't raining like a waterfall anymore. It was still pissin' down, but it wasn't blinding. "You all follow me back. No one goes faster than Silver, you understand? And keep your stupid hats on your heads."

17

MALLORY HAD RUN for the nearest barn, but when the heaviest rainfall had stopped, she'd joined Kathy and the other volunteers standing by the busted corral. Everyone was staring north, waiting.

She crossed her arms over her chest as if she could slow her racing heart. She needed some water, but she'd be damned if she was going to move. Gunner had acted so quickly it had taken her a while to understand he'd gone off to try to stop the kids from chasing after the mustangs.

"You okay?"

Mallory jumped at Kathy's voice. "I'm fine. I'm just—"

"That's one hell of a cowboy. That horse he got on is barely tame enough to saddle."

"He is— Wait. Is that—"

"I think so." Kathy was squinting hard at the approaching group, the kids loaded onto the ATVs, Gunner on the silver horse, leading them. His hat was cockeyed but you'd never know he didn't have a saddle under him. He looked damn good.

It took the group a minute to get to the barn, but when they finally were huddled together, the kids were all staring at Gunner like he was Iron Man or something.

"How'd you do that?" It was one of the drenched girls. They all looked like they'd been dragged out of a lake. "It was awesome."

"Totally. Like in the movies." This from a shivering blond boy. "I swear, it was like you voodooed the mustangs. Dammit, I wish I could have taped it. It would go viral on YouTube for sure!"

"Hey," Gunner said, his gravelly voice cutting through the chatter like a knife. "Shut it. All of you. That was not like the movies. You were all reckless in a dangerous situation. You don't chase wild horses and you don't get in their way. You stay as far away from them as you can. Remember what happened so you'll never do anything stupid like that again."

"But you—"

"I'm a professional stuntman. It took me years to be able to ride like that. Don't you go jumping on the next horse you see. You'll get creamed. Believe me. You're all so damn lucky nothing went seriously wrong. Spooked horses are nothing to mess with. Got it?"

They all nodded. Mallory barely looked at the kids. That speech from Gunner? She stared at him as if she'd been given a new pair of glasses. He looked like a drowned rat, and she'd never found him more appealing.

"And don't go talking about this when you go back to school. It might make some parents feel like they shouldn't let their kids come help out at Safe Haven. You don't want that, right?"

Another group nod.

Then Kathy took over, and Mallory couldn't wait to have Gunner to herself.

GOOD THING GUNNER'S truck had sturdy leather seats. They'd mopped themselves up as best they could but they were both pretty wet. Mallory rolled their soggy borrowed towels and glanced around for a place to stash them.

"Well, that was kind of weird," she said, deciding on the floorboard by her feet.

"Yeah, this being a ranching community you'd think those damn kids would have more sense."

"I meant you," she said. "The way you handled them. You even got that tall blond kid—you know which one, Mr. Hot Shit—to shut up and listen. You were awesome." She didn't care that he shook his head and looked mildly irritated. "How did you know what to say? Everything just came out so perfectly."

"Lucky, I guess."

"Nope. You don't get to be modest. Not with me. I wasn't the only one impressed, either. If Kathy wasn't old enough to be your mother, she would've married you on the spot."

That earned Mallory a wry smile.

She just laughed.

"Man, I was looking at those boys and thinking, was I ever that young?"

"Huh." She hadn't thought about it. "I'm not sure either of us were."

"Probably not," he said, and shrugged a shoulder.

"Do you want kids, Gunner?" She saw him stiffen and realized how easily the question could be misinterpreted. "What I mean is, have you ever thought about having your own kids?"

"Is there a difference between those two questions? Because I'm not seeing it."

"It popped into my head and I said it, okay?" She waited, disappointed that he'd made a joke instead of answering.

"You know I was a runaway," he said finally. "Hey, I wonder if that's the right term if the mom doesn't give a shit or doesn't even know her kid's missing."

Mallory swallowed at the hint of pain in his voice, or maybe she was projecting because of her own crappy childhood. Either way she was tempted to touch him, offer him some small measure of comfort. But she feared the odds were greater that he'd reject her and shut down. "You were fifteen when you left home, right?"

"Yep. Left town, left Texas. And whoever was the father du jour. Hell, I could pass any one of Luanne's boyfriends on the street and I wouldn't recognize him." He shrugged. "A couple were pretty decent guys. At least they treated me better than she did, which isn't saying much. So, yeah, I'd probably make a lousy father. No point putting a kid through that." He carefully kept his gaze on the road ahead. "What about you?"

Mallory shouldn't have been startled. Why wouldn't he ask her the same question? "I guess I haven't really thought about it," she said. "You knew Coop. As for my mom, consider yourself lucky you never met her. Two really great role models. I wouldn't know the first thing about raising kids."

Gunner smiled a little, and she wondered if she should tell him he was wrong about himself. He'd be a great dad. She'd just seen the evidence with her own eyes. In fact, she was beginning to realize there was a lot more to Gunner than she'd known.

"Have I ever mentioned Krista?" he asked, and Mallory shook her head. "She was a kid I met about a year after I got to LA. I was living rough, sleeping anywhere I could get away with, doing odd jobs for food. Krista was thirteen, naive and scared. She'd left home the week before I found her in an alley.

"I was sixteen by then, and knew how to get food when I didn't have money. And this poor kid, starving, getting no sleep because she was being hassled by some of the guys…" He shook his head, eyes staying focused on the road. "I told myself it wasn't my problem. Plenty of others like her. But I couldn't walk away. I even tried talking her into going back home until I found out her stepfather was abusive. So we started hanging out together. I shared my food with her, and when I was broke I stole a few apples and oranges, stuff like that."

Gunner tightened his mouth before releasing a harsh exhale. "I hated those times when it came down to stealing and I think she knew it. After two days of going without eating I told her to stay put while I got something from the corner grocer. She didn't listen. I suspected that she'd followed me into the store but I didn't do anything about it. She grabbed some candy bars right in front of the store's owner. He called the police and she was arrested. I vowed that day I would never be responsible for another human being again."

"Oh, my God, Gunner. You were sixteen." Mallory swallowed back a lump at the anguish in his face. She hated that the incident still haunted him. "Krista was lucky to have you."

"Yeah, right. I found out later she was sent back to her mom and stepfather." His hands tightened on the wheel. "I'd tried to protect her and I failed. They sent her right back to the bastard who was abusing her. I still think about her sometimes."

"I'm sure she thinks about you, too. How you'd shielded her from things that could've been so much worse." She sighed when he glanced at her with raised brows. "I'm not being naive. You know damn well she could've been terribly damaged. And who's to say she didn't end up in foster care or with another family member after social services figured out why she'd run away."

They'd reached town and lapsed into silence until they got to her street.

"The store owner who had her arrested turned out to be a pretty nice guy. I met him about eight years ago." A faint smile curved Gunner's mouth. "He knew kids had been stealing from him, but as long as they stuck to the little stuff and didn't grab two handfuls of candy bars right under his nose…" He shook his head. "If Krista hadn't been so bold Mr. Rawi would've looked the other way. He'd recently immigrated and knew what it was like to go hungry."

"How in the world did you run into him?"

"He still owns that same store on the corner. I dropped by one day to settle up. Confessed I'd shoplifted from him and gave him some money."

"Well, he must've been shocked."

Gunner laughed, looking more relaxed. "Yeah, he was, and damned if some little punk didn't try to sneak out with a bag of cookies while we were talking. Rawi made him put it back and threatened to call the police if he saw the boy again. He explained the kid wasn't homeless. Guess that was his criteria. Hell, I threw in another five hundred bucks to help with his losses."

"Wow, Gunner, that's an awesome story."

"Wish it had turned out better for Krista." He pulled the truck up to the curb near her gate.

"You don't know how that ended up," Mallory reminded him and scooped up the wet towels. She paused when he left the truck running. "Aren't you coming in?"

He glanced at the time.

"Unless you have somewhere else to be."

"Nope. Just don't want to make you late for work."

She leaned over and kissed him. "I'm the boss, remember? Now, come on. We could both use a hot shower."

That got his attention. With a slow smile he cut the engine.

"I CALLED ELAINE and it's all settled. She'll open up for me. We don't expect to be busy tonight, so I won't be going in till around eight. Oh, but I do have to run over in an hour to let the electrician in. Won't take long."

"Does Elaine have a key?"

"I gave her one yesterday."

That surprised Gunner. He continued to dry himself, aware that Mallory was leaning against the door frame with only a towel wrapped around her. But not for long. It was a damn crime to hide all those tempting female parts.

"You don't think I should've given her a key."

He glanced up. "Actually I was thinking about something else, but yeah, it's surprising since you've only known her for a few weeks."

"I suppose that's true. It's odd how trusting I've been lately. But the people around here are nice, Gunner. They really are." She seemed to glow with contentment but something nagged at him.

There was no question he was happy for her. She liked Blackfoot Falls and she was already making friends.

After her shitty childhood she deserved to have stability and security. And like she'd said, maybe she'd be able to have a life.

He tied the towel around his waist and, trying to get a handle on his scattered thoughts, turned to the mirror. It was completely fogged. Just like his befuddled brain. "I should've brought in my shaving kit," he murmured, rubbing his stubbled jaw.

"I can go get it for you," she said. "But if you're thinking about shaving for my benefit, don't bother."

"Would you please just stay in that towel? At least for a few more minutes."

Mallory grinned. "I'll drop mine when you drop yours."

He made a fake play for her that sent her jumping back and laughing.

Eyeing her legs while he cleared a spot on the mirror, he said, "I am so pissed it took me this long to find out you have great legs."

"Oh, yeah? If you'd known sooner what would you have done about it?"

Gunner smiled and combed his damp hair straight back.

He was about 95 percent certain he wanted to move to Blackfoot Falls and work with Ben. He just didn't understand why the 5 percent was holding him back. It had nothing to do with leaving Hollywood behind, that was for damn sure. But he was beginning to realize that it did have something to do with Mallory. She'd worried about disappointing him when he knew it should be the other way around. What if he couldn't be the man she needed? What if he failed her just like he'd failed Krista?

Dammit, why was he even thinking about the girl?

For the most part he'd made peace with what had happened back then. As Mallory had pointed out, he'd been a kid himself at the time. So no, he wouldn't let the past sabotage his future, if that's what his subconscious was trying to do.

But he was clear on one thing...he didn't want to screw up anything for Mallory. Maybe he simply needed to explain about the opportunity to work with Ben. Not tell her how close he was to a final decision. Just that there was a chance he could be moving to Blackfoot Falls.

Relief washed over him.

It was the best course of action he could think of without actually committing to anything or sinking in too deep.

He'd tell her in private. So he could see her face. Watch her reaction.

That first unguarded second would tell him a lot. It could reveal something she might not be comfortable admitting out loud. After all, when her car had run out of gas, her first instinct hadn't been to call him.

The possibility she didn't want him to stay twisted him up inside.

"Okay." He stripped off his towel and hung it on the rack. Telling her now wouldn't be right. She still had to go to the bar later. Tonight, after she closed, would be better. "Your turn."

The towel hit the floor before he'd finished speaking.

Her gaze slid down his body and briefly rested on his hardening cock. With a gentle smile she walked into his arms. He held her tight. And she hugged him back, as though she'd never let go.

She buried her face against his neck and sighed, her soft breath brushing his skin.

And just like that, the 5 percent of uncertainty disappeared. This was right. Her. Him. The two of them together. It didn't matter where. But if Blackfoot Falls made her happy, and she would have him, Gunner wasn't going anywhere.

MALLORY WAS RELIEVED to see Gunner walk into the bar at 10:30. Precisely when she'd expected him, so there'd been no reason for her to be anxious. She blamed the full moon for putting crazy thoughts in her head. Two customers had also caught the bug. Arguing over darts. So stupid. It reminded her of the Renegade.

Huh. She was thinking about the old place less these days. Of course she'd been too busy to be nostalgic. Or maybe it was because Gunner was here.

He sat at the other end since the stools by her were occupied by three older gentlemen. She finished pouring two whiskeys before she glanced over at him. All he did was wink and her heart fluttered. Damn, she really had it bad. Even worse since seeing him with the Safe Haven kids earlier.

Mallory should probably be worried. All fairy tales came to an end at some point. And hers would, too. She figured she'd wait until it happened and then be sad.

Oh, brother. She was so delusional.

Sadie's prediction had been spot-on. Business was slower than usual. Payday wasn't till the end of the week for the local hired hands, which had a lot to do with it. All in all, she couldn't complain. They'd had a decent crowd, thanks in part to some guys from the film crew who'd wandered in an hour ago.

Two of them were playing pool and flirting with a guest from the Sundance. The other two men were sitting at a table. She didn't think any of the guys were stuntmen.

Elaine was talking to one of her neighbors, an old-timer sitting by himself and nursing a beer. It didn't appear she'd need an order filled soon.

"You guys okay for now?" she asked the trio near her.

They all nodded, so she grabbed a rag and wiped the oak countertop as she made her way toward Gunner. He'd locked gazes with her and she'd be damned if she would look away first. Anyone trying to get her attention could get their own drink.

She stopped in front of him and watched one corner of his mouth slowly lift. "What can I do for you, cowboy?"

"Brave woman asking me that."

"Brave or stupid."

His gaze intensified, making her skin prickle.

"What?" she said, her mouth starting to go dry. "Stop it."

"You have any idea what I want to do to you right now?" He'd lowered his deep voice until it was gravelly and sexy, making her so hot that she wanted to crawl out of her own skin.

She hung in there, refusing to break eye contact, but he was so going to pay for this. Later. When she had him alone.

Jeez. She'd been holding her breath and didn't know it. When she finally exhaled, she sounded like a damn steam engine. This had to stop. "I have some good news," she said. "The electrician said the stage is almost ready. He has just one more thing to do. And the singer from Boot Stompin' called. They're starting next Friday night."

"That's great, sweetheart." His hand moved toward hers then stopped.

Dammit, she wanted to touch him, too. So why didn't she? "I don't know about a second night yet. We've agreed on two months to see how it works out for them to drive this far."

He glanced toward the back. "Is this the busiest you've been tonight?"

"We had about thirty customers at one point. I counted seventeen a few minutes ago."

"Not bad."

"Some of the crew from that miniseries are here. Camera guys maybe, but I'm not sure." She nodded at their table.

"Ah, shit."

"What? You know them I take it."

"The big guy in the tan shirt. I know him in passing. He's a stuntman. And a real hell-raiser when he drinks too much."

"I don't think he has so far."

"Hey, Ellison. Goddamn it, boy, is that you?"

Mallory winced. "Did I call attention to you? I'm sorry."

"It's fine. You didn't do anything." Gunner lifted a hand in acknowledgment.

"Well, get over here and I'll buy you a drink." He had a booming voice that seemed to bounce off every surface.

Gunner didn't respond until the big guy stood. "Hold on, Jenkins. I'll be over in a minute."

"Leave if you want," Mallory said, feeling as if this

was somehow her fault. "I can meet you at the house later."

"It's okay. I'll have a beer with him if it'll keep his big mouth shut."

"Why? Don't do it for me. Ignore him, Gunner."

He gave her another private wink. "It's okay. Promise."

She watched him head to the table, a weird feeling of foreboding tightening her chest. It was crazy. There was no basis for it. And then she noticed one of the customers sitting at the bar motioning to her. "Do you want another whiskey?" she asked.

"Yes, ma'am. But this will be my last one," he said, pushing his empty glass toward her. "And if my wife calls, you just tell her you didn't see me all night. You hear?"

Mallory smiled at the mischief in his faded blue eyes. "Since I don't know your name that shouldn't be hard to do."

"He's just pullin' your leg. Clem ain't even married." His friend elbowed him. "No woman in her right mind would have him."

"I don't know," Mallory drawled. "A nice-looking man like him, I bet the women line up to bring him supper on Sundays."

Clem hooted. "You hear that, Lester?" he said to his friend who choked out a laugh. Clem leaned closer as she set his drink down. "Honey, I'd never make you wait in line."

They all laughed at that. Then Lester said, "What would she want with an old coot like you when she's got that big strapping young man who's gonna be Ben Wolf's new partner?"

Mallory must've misheard him. "Who are you talking about?"

"Your fella over there." Lester nodded in Gunner's direction. "The sheriff told me about it. You know Grace?"

Clem swung him a look. "You don't know the sheriff. Just because she says hi to you don't mean nothing."

"Oh, all right. I overheard her and that fella talking when he was getting things set up at the bank."

Mallory was vaguely aware of the two men bickering about Clem putting on airs, but she felt light-headed and couldn't seem to breathe. She told herself there had to be more to the story. Or that the older man was confused. But flashing back to several odd comments, too much of it already made sense. But how could he do this to her?

Gunner. Living in Blackfoot Falls? He'd never last. And when he left for good, she'd be...shattered.

18

"GET MY BUDDY here a drink and put it on my tab," Jenkins hollered at Elaine even before Gunner sat down. "Would ya do that for me, darlin'?"

She glanced at Gunner, frowning as if she wasn't sure what to do.

He shook his head. "Nothing for me, Elaine. I'm not drinking tonight."

"You call yourself a stuntman? Not drinking," Jenkins muttered. "That's bullshit. Bring him a shot."

Gunner ignored the ignorant bastard.

The other guy sitting at the table introduced himself as Bruce. Whether or not he was okay with the loudmouth wasn't clear. But he seemed relieved when Gunner took a seat.

"So what the hell you doing way up here in this shit hole, Ellison?" Jenkins glanced toward the bar. "Besides hitting on that pretty bartender."

"We're friends." Gunner kept his voice low, hoping the idiot got the message to leave Mallory alone. "Mal and I go way back."

"Just friends, huh?" He twisted around to get another look. "So you wouldn't mind if I hit that."

Gunner bit down hard. He flexed his hands to keep them from fisting. Then he did the only thing he knew to do without causing a load of trouble. He laughed.

Jenkins stared blankly at him.

"So what? You guys are working on the miniseries?" Gunner looked from Jenkins to Bruce, who seemed eager to answer when Jenkins cut him off.

"What the hell were you laughing at?" He stared at Gunner the whole time he drained his beer.

"I laugh at jokes."

"Is that right?" The bastard frowned. "Why would you think I was joking?"

Gunner laughed again. "Christ, Jenkins, she's so far out of your league all you'd do is make an ass out of yourself."

Jenkins's eyes got mean. He leaned across the table toward Gunner. "Just because you're too stupid to fuck her doesn't mean I am."

Bruce twitched and bumped the big man's shoulder. "Come on, Jenkins, let's get out of here."

"Get off." He jabbed his elbow hard into Bruce's ribs. But Jenkins kept Gunner in his sights and Gunner was fine with that. "Maybe you're scared of women. Maybe I should go show her how a real man does it."

Elaine approached, glaring. "Okay, that's enough—"

Gunner waved her back. "I'm going to tell you as nicely as I can, and only once. You need to settle up and leave."

"Fuck you." Jenkins turned to Elaine and demanded another drink.

Bruce got to his feet. "We're outta here," he said to

the two men coming from the back room. "You don't come with us now, Jenkins, you're walking."

"I ain't leaving until I get me a piece of that blonde's ass," he said, taunting Gunner with a smug grin.

"Okay." Gunner scraped back his chair and stood. He'd hoped the guy's buddies would've stepped in and convinced Jenkins to leave. But they were all standing back, watching.

Gunner wouldn't look at Mallory. He knew she was still behind the bar, so that was good. No telling what she'd heard, though.

Elaine stepped in front of him. "I called the deputy. He should be here soon."

Soon wasn't soon enough for a guy like Jenkins. "Thanks, Elaine," Gunner said. "You'd better stay out of the way now."

With a small, resigned shake of her head, she moved back.

Gunner stood in front of Jenkins. "You're really going to make me do this."

Jenkins snarled, his right hand already forming into a fist. "You can try, boy."

Gunner grabbed the front of his shirt and yanked him out of the chair. Shit. The son of a bitch weighed a ton. Jenkins took a swing but it went wide and Gunner barely had to duck.

"Come on, let's go," Gunner said, so damn tempted to clock the asshole. Five years ago he wouldn't have thought twice about throwing a punch. But all he wanted now was to drag him toward the door and avoid damaging anything.

Jenkins cursed him up one side and down the other. The bastard was heavy as hell and trying to knock Gunner's head off. When Jenkins kicked a chair over, that was it. Luckily, they'd gotten as far as the dance floor. Gunner stopped and punched Jenkins. He landed flat on his back.

What a pussy. Gunner hadn't hit him all that hard but he was out cold.

He looked at Mallory then. "You want to press charges or let his friends take him?"

She looked pale. And angry, sad and helpless all at once. The place had practically cleared except for the three old codgers sitting at the bar with their jaws in their laps. Was she upset about that? Did she blame him that people had left?

"I just want him out of here," she said so softly he barely heard. Something in her tone sent a razor-sharp zing down his spine, and he wanted everyone gone. Now.

Bruce and the other two finally dragged Jenkins out the door.

Gunner walked past Mallory and the three old guys with their ears primed, and waited for her to join him at the other end.

She moved slowly, her head down, stopping about three feet away. "You too," she said, her voice low and shaky as she looked into his eyes. "You have to go."

"Mallory…"

She shook her head, and he saw she was trembling.

"I tried my best not to throw a punch, but I had to make him leave before he started breaking things."

"It doesn't matter." She gestured at the sign behind her.

No Fighting, or You Will Be Banned.

She'd been staring at him when he met her gaze. "You can't be serious," he said, trying to keep his voice down.

"I am. I can't start making exceptions." Her dismissive shrug pissed him off. But something else was going on. Anger simmered in her eyes, turning them a fiery green. "Shouldn't be a problem. It's not as if you live here. You'll be leaving soon, right?"

Jesus. His gut clenched. The way she'd said it, he knew she'd heard about him partnering with Ben. Gunner had no idea what or how much she knew, only that she knew something. It seemed impossible since he'd just finalized the decision today. But then again, this was typical small-town bullshit. A flicker of gossip or news always managed to spread like wildfire.

"Oh, wait. Maybe you aren't going anywhere." Mallory glared at him as though she hated his guts. "Maybe you plan on—"

"I was going to tell you tonight. I swear it," he said, tempted to kick out the nosy old geezers trying their best to listen. "Can we go to your house and talk?"

"I'm working. You have to leave. We have nothing to talk about." Mallory lifted her chin. "I believe that covers everything."

"You have to let me explain." Sweat dampened the back of his neck. But a tiny bit of hope flared when she moved farther away from the old guys.

"No explanation necessary. You wanted sex," she said in a hushed voice. "I agreed because I thought you'd be gone soon. You got what you wanted, so—" Her voice broke. "Just go."

"The thing is," he said, holding on to his own temper, "I don't just cut and run. I might screw up but I stick around long enough to explain myself."

Mallory looked startled at first. Then, her expression softened for a moment…before she lowered her lashes, as though she couldn't bear to look at him. "Go back to California," she said, her voice barely above a whisper and as distant as the Rockies.

IT FIGURED SHE'D run out of tissues at 4:45 in the morning. With the brisk mountain air cooling the house she should have been snuggled under the covers, sound asleep. Not crying and wiping her nose, wishing last night had been nothing but a bad dream.

Mallory grabbed a roll of toilet paper and took it with her to her bedroom. Her gaze fell on Gunner's pillow and she felt a stab of longing.

Screw that. It wasn't his pillow because he would never spend the night in her bed again. In fact, if she never laid eyes on him again it would be fine. No... great. Perfect even.

She'd had to hear about his future plans from a complete stranger? And not just any plans. He had to know how much a move to Blackfoot Falls would impact her.

Stupid ass.

Did he think she would've cut him off if she'd known he was going to stay? Was the sex more important to him than being honest with her? The thought of it made her stomach clench.

Ben hadn't said a word, either. Grace could've hinted, though. Didn't women have some kind of unspoken sisterhood thing going on? But what did Mallory know? Except how to pour drinks.

And dammit, she'd thought she knew Gunner.

Apparently not.

The guilty look on his face when she'd confronted him wasn't about to fade from her memory anytime soon. God, she was stupid. If she'd been listening instead of walking around in a haze of lust she would've wised up. Those weird remarks she'd blown off? Had she willfully ignored every single sign?

Had she really believed that just because Gunner had been good with those kids he'd be the kind of man who'd stick around?

Except that he *was* sticking around, or had planned to, and that's what confused her.

She took a deep shuddering breath and something seemed to shake loose in her brain. She'd been too obsessed thinking sex was the reason he hadn't told her and had overlooked the obvious answer.

He couldn't be completely sure moving to Blackfoot Falls was the right thing to do. And he never would be sure. This wasn't the life for him. He'd get bored. Maybe he'd last a few months or even a year, but he would eventually tire of the monotony, grow tired of her. Hell, maybe he'd even resent her.

She was partly to blame. She'd actually begun to think sex could make their relationship stronger. Take them from friendship to a deeper intimacy.

What relationship? She sniffed, tearing off a piece of toilet paper. She was better off alone.

Maybe she'd get a dog. A cat might be easier.

Damn, she couldn't even figure out who she hated more, Gunner or herself.

She blew her nose, then stilled when she thought she heard her phone. At 5:00 a.m.?

Gunner. He'd left angry. Had he been in an—

Her heart nearly exploded as she ran to answer her cell.

"Mallory?" It was Sadie. "First, don't get upset, but there's been a small fire at the Full Moon—"

It took her four minutes to wash her face, get dressed and find her car keys, her stomach churning the whole time. The moment she opened her front door she smelled smoke. She hadn't seen any flames, though, not from her house or even when she turned onto Main Street.

She parked several yards behind the big old fire truck and opened her door, the acrid stench of burning embers filling her sinuses. Several onlookers were huddled on the street. Sadie was standing on the sidewalk talking to two firemen. Mallory stepped around a huge coiled hose to get to them.

The Full Moon's wooden door was open and she told herself not to look inside as she passed. She did anyway. Her father's chairs and tables, the new stage, all a charred mess.

"Let's talk. You can look later." Sadie was suddenly beside her, gently steering her toward the firemen.

The short older man gave her a sympathetic nod when Sadie introduced him as Grover. Mallory didn't recognize him. The younger man had sat at the bar the other night. He drank Coors.

"Before we—" She cleared her throat. "Please, tell me, is the bakery okay?" She saw their puzzled looks. "It's not open yet but we share a wall..."

"It's fine," Sadie said, squeezing her hand. "The fire—"

Mallory put up a hand. "Did I cause it? Was I careless?"

"No." Grover jumped in, all business. "It was an electrical fire that started behind the stage. I know you've been renovating but have you had any recent work done?"

She nodded. "Yesterday," she said, barely able to get the word out. She owned the bar. It was still her fault.

"Cecil?" Sadie asked.

"Yes, but—"

"Nobody is saying he did it on purpose." Sadie smiled. "Accidents happen. That's why we have insurance."

Mallory briefly closed her eyes and swallowed.

"You must have insurance." Sadie looked worried.

"I do. With a huge deductible. I planned on changing the policy later after I started making a profit." Her voice broke.

"Luckily, you don't have any structural damage," Grover said. "We caught the fire early thanks to Boyd Meacham, who was letting his dog out. I'll know more in the next hour, but it shouldn't take much to get you back on your feet."

"Thanks, Grover," Sadie said.

All Mallory could do was nod. No, it might not take much, but having nothing was still nothing. And she didn't even have Gunner's shoulder to cry on. It didn't matter.

She stood outside the Full Moon, just staring, shocked beyond tears.

19

AT 7:45 A.M. GUNNER heard the news from Grace and by 7:50 he was in his truck speeding toward town. It made him sick to think Mallory hadn't called him herself. Sure, they'd had words last night, and he was still pissed about things she'd said. But it wasn't as though she'd stubbed her toe, or run out of gas again. Her bar had caught on goddamn fire and she hadn't called him?

Naturally he'd tried her cell but she hadn't answered, and damned if that hadn't pushed all kinds of buttons.

A bunch of trucks and cars lined the street and he had to park four blocks away but it was probably for the best. There was so much crap going on in his head that a walk might help. Some of his anger still lingered but he hadn't given up hope.

He'd done a lot of thinking about him staying and why he hadn't told her yet. And yeah, he still deserved an explanation regarding her disappearing act. But Gunner had figured they would take a couple days to cool off, then have a frank conversation. Work out whatever they needed to.

Yesterday, he'd been optimistic enough to have told

Ben they had a deal and then, while Mallory had met with the electrician, Gunner had dashed to the bank and had some good-faith money wired. Ben had said it was completely unnecessary, but Gunner figured the cash deposit on their new partnership could be used to get some improvements under way.

If it had turned out Gunner still had to prove he was the man she needed, he'd decided he was willing to do that. Right now, he wasn't sure how he felt.

Jesus, there were a lot of people swarming outside the Full Moon. Some were wearing bathrobes, but most of the folks were in work clothes and hauling charred pieces of wood out of the bar and loading them onto trucks.

As he got closer he realized they were the tables and chairs Mallory had from Coop. His insides tightened. They weren't worth much, but she had a sentimental streak when it came to the few things her father had passed on to her.

A guy he vaguely recognized from the other night stopped to shift his hold on a chair. "Don't worry, Gunner. We got lots of folks pitching in. We'll have Mallory back in business in no time."

Gunner managed a small nod. Most of these people barely knew her. She hadn't been here long enough. But that hadn't stopped them from rallying to her rescue. He scanned the crowd and saw two women carrying trays of muffins and doughnuts that they set on a folding table next to pots of coffee. He hadn't spotted Mallory yet so he moved to the door.

She was leaning against the bar, her hair a wild mess around her pale face. Mostly she kept her head down, nodding at something the man with his arm around her was saying. Gunner recognized him right away. Mike. The guy from that first night. Whatever he was whispering to Mallory brought some color to her cheeks and a small smile to her lips.

Gunner doubted he had a single goddamn thing to say that would comfort her—unless him returning to California made her day.

But that's not what he'd decided he was going to do. He wanted to fight for her. Fight for her trust. For her love.

Brady, the guy who'd helped with Fanny, stopped to give Mallory a reassuring pat on her back. She gave him a smile that would melt any man's heart. Other men Gunner had seen at the bar, and some he hadn't, were giving her words of encouragement or reassuring nods as they worked to clean up the debris.

While he stood back, waiting, watching, twisted up with indecision, he heard two women talking about how Mallory had pledged money from her beer sales to Kyle Higgins's medical care. And wasn't that nice of her, Mallory being a newcomer and all?

Gunner remembered the collection jar she'd placed on the bar. Whether or not it was common practice for businesses to collect donations, it hadn't surprised him that Mallory had chipped in, then gone the extra mile. She was a good person with a kind heart, despite being born to two selfish jerks who hadn't given a shit about her.

In a short time she'd become a part of the community. Not because she'd gone out of her way to be accepted. Blackfoot Falls had welcomed her because of the type of person she was, pure and simple. She fit in here.

And he didn't.

For most of his life Gunner had felt as if he was standing on the outside looking in. Even after he'd become a stuntman and joined the Association and the union. He'd gotten along okay with most everyone, but a distance had always existed between him and them. He'd remained an outsider. But he'd never felt that way with Mallory.

Not until right now.

She had all the help and comfort she needed. Deserved. What the hell did he have to offer her? It was pretty damn clear she didn't need him. In fact, she would be better off without him.

In the middle of talking to a young man wearing a T-shirt that read Fire and Rescue, she reached into her pocket. When she brought out her cell and answered a call, Gunner's heart took the final plunge to the pit of his stomach.

He'd been clinging to a shred of hope that she'd misplaced her phone in the confusion and that's why she hadn't answered his calls. Now he knew better.

He stepped back, knowing she hadn't seen him. He was wrong about not having anything to offer. She wanted two things he could provide. First he had to stop at the bank and pick up the money he'd had wired. Then he'd head back to LA, just as she'd asked him to do.

If he'd been thinking rationally, he would've remembered that she'd run away from him. Mallory had never wanted him here in the first place.

It was just past 10:00 when Gunner finished writing the second note. The first had been an apology to Ben. Hell, he hoped his friend would understand. The second note, though, had been much harder to write. The wadded-up balls of paper around him testified to that. This version, though? He'd taken out all the angry stuff. Just told her that he hoped the money would help her fix the bar and that he'd miss her. He'd signed it with a plain goodbye.

Ben had left to deliver horses and wouldn't be back until evening. That was perfect. Gunner had time to make a clean getaway. After one last look around the guest room, he grabbed his duffel bag and went to the kitchen. It didn't take but a minute to leave the envelopes and the sticky note instructions on the cherry table and head out to his truck.

His heart hadn't merely sunk to his stomach back in town. He'd left it there on the sidewalk, battered and broken. This whole thing was on him. He'd known better than to get attached. Than to think he could be a man Mallory could count on.

Even so it took a lot more than a minute for him to turn the key. But in the end, he did.

A GIRL WHO worked at the coffee shop had shoved a fresh coffee at Mallory, which she'd taken, although she'd been trembling from head to toe. Everything about the morning felt surreal. All these people who'd come to help? She barely knew them. Some she'd never seen before. She was grateful beyond words, but she was also in shock. Not just about the fire or her neighbors. Gunner hadn't shown up. She'd thought for sure—

"Hey, kiddo. How you holding up?"

She turned at Ben's voice behind her. "I'm here," she said, her voice gruff from more than smoke and no sleep. "I thought you were gone for the day."

"I came back as soon as Grace got ahold of me." He stood beside her, watching people hustle in and out of the bar.

"You shouldn't have. There's nothing you can do."

"Come on," he said, squeezing her shoulder. "You think I could've stayed away?"

Why not? Gunner had no problem avoiding her. So they hadn't parted on good terms last night. She never would've dreamed he'd let that get in the way considering what had happened to the bar.

"They won't let me help." She saw the envelope in his hand and a bad feeling crept over her.

"They're good folks," he said, nodding slowly. "Come over here with me for a minute." He took her arm and steered them to a more private spot by the new bakery.

Mallory knew it was going to be bad. Knew it in every cell of her being. She was amazed her legs were holding up.

"He wanted me to give you this," Ben said, passing her the thick envelope.

She took it, the heft of it making her curious. But the bad feeling persisted. Her hands trembled so hard Ben had to open the envelope for her. It was filled with cash. "What the hell?"

Ben blew out a breath. "Should be about fifteen grand there. A deposit for his share of the ranch. He probably figured you'd tear up a check."

She bit down on her lip. "Where is he?" she asked, though she was certain she knew.

"Gone."

Already knowing didn't help at all. Turned out she still had a few more tears left inside her.

"Listen, it's none of my business, but Gunner, he wanted to tell you about staying."

A flare of anger set her off. "So basically, everyone knew that but me."

"He only decided yesterday." Ben paused. Indecision darkened his eyes. "He had a reason he didn't tell you."

Something in those words made Mallory's heart change rhythm.

"He was worried."

"About what?"

Ben looked at his boots. "That he wasn't good enough for you. That you didn't feel you could count on him."

It was like being hit by a truck. Mallory's whole body cringed. "Why? How could he possibly think that?"

She hadn't realized how loud her voice had gotten until Grace moved in and put a hand on her shoulder. "For what it's worth, Gunner was here earlier."

"Here?" Mallory asked. "This morning?"

Grace nodded. "He was standing at the door when I was trying to get the crowd to give the workers some room. I figured he'd work his way to you eventually but when I looked again, he'd disappeared."

"I didn't see him." Mallory stared at her phone. "I wondered why he hadn't called..." She checked and saw that he had... No messages, though. "There was so much noise and confusion—"

"He probably didn't count on Ben coming back this early and finding the notes," Grace said.

Mallory just stared at her, trying to make sense of things. "How long ago did he leave?"

"I'm guessing about an hour, maybe less."

Mallory sighed. It might as well have been a week. She doubted she was even capable of driving.

"You know, I've got a siren and a fast truck," Grace whispered. "If you want, I bet we can catch him."

Hope ran through Mallory like sweet water. "I want," she said, and nothing had ever been truer.

Grace started for her truck, and Mallory practically ran to the passenger side and got in. That's when she looked past the money to the note Gunner had left her. By the time they were on the highway, the siren parting the sparse traffic like the Red Sea, Mallory had used up all of Grace's tissues, and started wiping her eyes with the bottom of her shirt.

"REALLY?" GUNNER COULDN'T believe he was being pulled over. Today of all days. He just reached over to the glove box and pulled out his registration as he opened his window. When he looked up again, Mallory was standing next to his truck, her hands on her hips, her eyes bloodshot.

"Come on out of there," she said.

He looked in the rearview to see Grace standing by her vehicle. So it must not have been a hallucination. He stepped out of the truck, pulling Mallory to the side, away from the highway. "What are you doing?"

"Give me the keys, Gunner."

"Why?"

"Just do it."

He sighed, reached in and grabbed the keys from the ignition, only to have Mallory toss them over to Grace, who made a great catch.

"You got the handcuffs ready if he gives me a hard time?"

Grace held them up, the sun glinting off her aviator sunglasses.

Rubbing his tired eyes, he sighed again. What the hell went wrong? Grace must've gotten to the envelopes first. He hadn't anticipated that.

"You are so stupid, Gunner."

"Tell me something I don't know."

"Okay," Mallory said. "I love you. Though you should already know that, too."

He wasn't at all prepared for her to grab him by his shirt and pull him into a kiss. And it was one hell of a kiss. He felt it all the way to the worry that had tied his gut in knots, to his hands that pulled her into his arms. To his heart, which was beating with a joy he could barely contain.

When she broke the kiss, it was only to meet his gaze with a glare. "Why would you run off like this? I'm so pissed at you. You leave me a wad of cash and take off? What's wrong with you?"

"Too many things to count," he said, "but—"

"Don't say it. Don't you dare say it. You're the best man, the most wonderful man I've ever met. I will not let you break my heart. Do you hear me?" She gulped in a breath. "And dammit, I know you love me, too. And if you ever, ever make a comment about not being good enough, I'll… I'll…love you harder. As hard as I have to. Understand?"

He nodded as he pulled her tight. This time, he kissed her. With all the mush he could muster. People were honking their horns, but he ignored everyone and everything around them.

Finally he pulled back to look into her eyes. "I do love you, sweetheart. I have for a while, even when I didn't know what love really meant."

The tender way she was looking back at him brought a lump to his throat.

"I have one request," she said, holding his gaze.

"Anything."

"If you ever start getting restless or decide that living in Blackfoot Falls isn't what you want, you have to tell me. No holding back."

It was an easy answer. "I give you my word," he said, touching her cheek. "When I came back from Argentina and you weren't there…" Remembering, he drew in a deep breath. "I never want to feel that void again. I don't care where I live or what I'm doing as long as I'm with you."

Her smile filled any tiny empty places left in his heart. But as he leaned in to steal another kiss he realized the Blackfoot Falls sheriff's truck was gone. "Did Grace take off with my keys?"

Mallory turned and laughed. "She'll figure it out and come back at some point."

"Well," Gunner said, "as long as we've got the time, you want to get inside the truck and make out?"

Mallory sighed. "That's a perfect idea," she said and they started kissing again, before he could get the door open.

* * * * *

COMING NEXT MONTH FROM

HARLEQUIN *Blaze*

Available May 24, 2016

#895 COWBOY ALL NIGHT
Thunder Mountain Brotherhood
by Vicki Lewis Thompson

When Aria Danes hires a legendary horse trainer to work with her new foal, she isn't expecting sexy, easygoing Brant Ellison. But when they're together, it's too hot for either to maintain their cool!

#896 A SEAL'S DESIRE
Uniformly Hot!
by Tawny Weber

Petty Officer Christian "Cowboy" Laramie is the hero Sammie Jo Wilson always looked up to. When she needs his help, she finds out she is the only woman Laramie thinks is off-limits...but for how long?

#897 TURNING UP THE HEAT
Friends With Benefits
by Tanya Michaels

Pastry chef Phoebe Mars and sophisticated charmer Heath Jensen are only pretending to date in order to make Phoebe's ex jealous. But there's nothing pretend about the sexy heat between them!

#898 IN THE BOSS'S BED
by J. Margot Critch

Separating business and pleasure proves to be impossible for Maya Connor and Jamie Sellers. When they can't keep their passion out of the boardroom, scandal threatens to destroy everything they've worked for.

REQUEST YOUR FREE BOOKS!
2 FREE NOVELS PLUS 2 FREE GIFTS!

(H) HARLEQUIN®

Blaze®
red-hot reads!

YES! Please send me 2 FREE Harlequin® Blaze® novels and my 2 FREE gifts (gifts are worth about $10). After receiving them, if I don't wish to receive any more books, I can return the shipping statement marked "cancel." If I don't cancel, I will receive 4 brand-new novels every month and be billed just $4.74 per book in the U.S. or $5.21 per book in Canada. That's a savings of at least 14% off the cover price. It's quite a bargain. Shipping and handling is just 50¢ per book in the U.S. and 75¢ per book in Canada.* I understand that accepting the 2 free books and gifts places me under no obligation to buy anything. I can always return a shipment and cancel at any time. Even if I never buy another book, the two free books and gifts are mine to keep forever.

150/350 HDN GH2D

Name	(PLEASE PRINT)

Address	Apt. #

City	State/Prov.	Zip/Postal Code

Signature (if under 18, a parent or guardian must sign)

Mail to the **Reader Service:**
IN U.S.A.: P.O. Box 1867, Buffalo, NY 14240-1867
IN CANADA: P.O. Box 609, Fort Erie, Ontario L2A 5X3

Want to try two free books from another line?
Call 1-800-873-8635 or visit www.ReaderService.com.

* Terms and prices subject to change without notice. Prices do not include applicable taxes. Sales tax applicable in N.Y. Canadian residents will be charged applicable taxes. Offer not valid in Quebec. This offer is limited to one order per household. Not valid for current subscribers to Harlequin Blaze books. All orders subject to credit approval. Credit or debit balances in a customer's account(s) may be offset by any other outstanding balance owed by or to the customer. Please allow 4 to 6 weeks for delivery. Offer available while quantities last.

Your Privacy—The Reader Service is committed to protecting your privacy. Our Privacy Policy is available online at www.ReaderService.com or upon request from the Reader Service.

We make a portion of our mailing list available to reputable third parties that offer products we believe may interest you. If you prefer that we not exchange your name with third parties, or if you wish to clarify or modify your communication preferences, please visit us at www.ReaderService.com/consumerchoice or write to us at Reader Service Preference Service, P.O. Box 9062, Buffalo, NY 14240-9062. Include your complete name and address.

He longed to reach for her, but instead he leaned into the van and snagged her hat. "You'll need this."

"Thanks." She settled the hat on her head—instant sexy cowgirl. "Let's go."

Somehow he managed to stop looking at her long enough to put his feet in motion. No doubt about it, he was hooked on her, and they'd only met yesterday.

If she was aware of his infatuation, she didn't let on as they walked into the barn. "I'm excited that we'll be taking him out today. I thought he might have to stay inside a little longer."

"Only if the weather had been nasty. But it's gorgeous." Like *you*. He'd almost said that out loud. Talk about cheesy compliments. "Cade and I already turned the other horses out into the far pasture, but we kept these two in the barn. We figured you should be here for Linus's big moment."

"Thank goodness you waited for me. I would have been crushed if I'd missed this."

"I wouldn't have let that happen." Okay, he was grandstanding a little, but it was true. Nobody at the ranch would have allowed Aria to miss watching Linus experience his first time outside.

"How about Rosie and Herb? Will they come watch?"

"You couldn't keep them away. A foal's first day in the pasture is special. Lexi and Cade are up at the house having breakfast with them, so they'll all come down in a bit." And he'd text them so they'd know she was here.

But not yet. He didn't foresee a lot of opportunities to be alone with her unless he created them. He wanted to savor this moment for a little while longer.

"Brant, can I ask a favor?" She paused and turned to him.

"Sure." He stopped walking.

Taking off her hat, she stepped toward him. "Would you please kiss me?"

With a groan he swept her up into his arms so fast she squeaked in surprise and his hat fell off…again. His mouth found hers and he thrust his tongue deep. His hands slid around her and when he lifted her up, she gave a little hop and wrapped her legs around his hips. Dear God, it felt good to wedge himself between her thighs.

Don't miss COWBOY ALL NIGHT
by New York Times *bestselling author*
Vicki Lewis Thompson, available June 2016 wherever
Harlequin® Blaze® books and ebooks are sold.

www.Harlequin.com

Whatever You're Into… Passionate Reads

Looking for more passionate reads from Harlequin®?
Fear not! Harlequin® Presents, Harlequin® Desire and
Harlequin® Blaze offer you irresistible romance stories
featuring powerful heroes.

♦HARLEQUIN *Presents*.

Do you want alpha males, decadent glamour and jet-set
lifestyles? Step into the sensational, sophisticated world of
Harlequin® Presents, where sinfully tempting heroes ignite a
fierce and wickedly irresistible passion!

♦HARLEQUIN *Desire*

Harlequin® Desire novels are powerful, passionate and
provocative contemporary romances set against a backdrop of
wealth, privilege and sweeping family saga. Alpha heroes with
a soft side meet strong-willed but vulnerable heroines amid a
dramatic world of divided loyalties, high-stakes conflict and
intense emotion.

♦HARLEQUIN *Blaze*.

Harlequin® Blaze stories sizzle with strong heroines and
irresistible heroes playing the game of modern love and lust.
They're fun, sexy and always steamy.

Be sure to check out our full selection of books
within each series every month!

www.Harlequin.com